MIKE VAN WAES

PEEVES

HarperCollins Children's Books

First published in the USA by HarperCollins Publishers, Inc. in 2018
First published in Great Britain by HarperCollins *Children's Books* in 2018
HarperCollins *Children's Books* is a division of HarperCollins *Publishers* Ltd,
HarperCollins Publishers
1 London Bridge Street
London SE1 9GF

The HarperCollins website address is:
www.harpercollins.co.uk

1

ISBN 978–0–00–824912–0

Typeset by Palimpsest Book Production Limited, Falkirk, Stirlingshire
Printed and bound in England by CPI Group (UK) Ltd, Croydon, CR0 4YY

MIX
Paper from
responsible sources
FSC® C007454

To Madison, Jack and Evie —
it's a big life; try not to let the
little things bug you.

PROLOGUE:

THE END

I'm not going to start at the beginning because that would be my birth and it's probably gross and boring and I don't actually remember it. And I'll also save you the full "origin story" of my superhuman ability to be freaked out. The "previously on" version is that I woke up one night two years ago and I felt like I couldn't breathe. I started dry-heaving and sweating and crying and shaking. I was so convinced I was dying that my parents rushed me to the ER. When the doctor saw me, she literally laughed in my face. "It was just a panic attack." As if that made it feel any less like a near-death experience. With the scribble of a pen and a rip off a prescription pad, she assured me it would most likely be a one-time thing. But those sounds are something I've been very used to hearing ever since.

And I still wake up in a panic some nights. Except now I'm in a different home. Or homes, really, because the divorce ended with two of them. And even though that went down a few months ago, it's just one more trigger for the panic to pull. Once I start to worry, it's only a matter of time. And so many things make me worry. It can start with a comment or an irritation or even a noise or a smell, and then I'm off. I can't stop it. "You're too young to be so stressed out," is what my parents would say. But any twelve-year-old can tell you that grown-ups don't have a monopoly on grown-up feelings. That is, if any twelve-year-old were willing to talk about it. That was one of my problems. Maybe my biggest problem.

But that was before the "incident" in Old Wayford. Before the end of life as I knew it.

And that ending actually begins with my name.

CHAPTER 1

THE LAB RATS

"Are you Steve?" came a surprisingly pleasant voice.

It was the first day at my new school, I was sitting in the principal's office, waiting to be shown around, and I was trying to decide which seat I should get used to just in case I wound up being sent to the office as much as I did at my last school. It's bad enough being new, but I was also transferring mid-semester, which is kind of like walking into the middle of a movie and not knowing any of the setup. My leg was bouncing uncontrollably, a clear sign that I was anxious about being dragged around by some random kid who would have to pretend to be nice to me all day.

I was predicting that I'd be completely abandoned by third period.

But then I heard my name called.

I looked up to see a smile.

A real smile. Not a "grown-ups are making me do this" smile.

"I'm Suzie. Suzie Minkle. Welcome to New Old Wayford Middle School!"

My face flushed and my throat closed up before I could even croak out a mumbled, "Slim Pickings."

She cocked her head curiously, which made her dark, natural curls bounce like they were alive and excited to be there. Then she laughed, but not at my expense. "I guess you have a point. It's not like there are a lot of schools to go to in town."

I blinked at her as if trying to clear floaters from my eyes. Suzie was one of only a handful of black kids I'd seen walking into this school, but if she felt the slightest bit like an outsider, I couldn't tell. She was wearing a Twenty One Pilots T-shirt under a blue mesh cover-up with yoga trousers and red Doc Martens. The whole look gave her a cool, relaxed vibe that made her seem at ease in ways I didn't know existed. And man did she smell nice. I had no idea what it was, but whatever soap or perfume or shampoo she used, it was literally a breath of fresh air. "No. It's my name. S-S-Slim," I stuttered as I followed her into the hall.

And believe it or not, she smiled when I said that. "Slim – that's a cool name. Mine sounds like an annoying neighbour on a sitcom, but that's okay. I'm used to it."

Despite my trouble talking like a human, Suzie made me feel like I belonged. Which is something I never felt at my last school – or anywhere else, really. The funny thing about Suzie is that she genuinely wants to be friends with everyone. "My dads own a yoga and wellness centre in town, so I think it's important to be centred and mindful, don't you?" I liked the sound of those soothing words strung together, even if I didn't understand what she meant. So I nodded. I wanted to agree because I wanted her to keep smiling. Normally I'd find it strange for someone to seem so obviously, outwardly happy. I'd overanalyse what it means and what she's hiding and wonder if she's making fun of me. But somehow Suzie made it work. I guess happiness can be a genuine thing. Imagine that.

Instead of going straight to homeroom, Suzie gave me a tour of the whole school so I would know my way around. And as we walked the halls or popped our heads into the library, cafeteria and gym, she greeted everyone we saw by telling them, "This is Slim. He's new and interesting." I'd never seen anything like it before: everyone liked her. I liked her. In fact, I pretty much instantly "like-liked" her. There's no point in pretending I didn't because you'll figure it out, and even if you didn't, my sister Lucy would tell you. She's a total blabbermouth; she'll do anything to get a little attention.

But at the time, walking the halls in New Old Wayford Middle School, with Suzie Minkle treating me like a normal human being, it felt like maybe I wouldn't have to be the freak at this school. Maybe I wouldn't have any meltdowns. I even made it through most of my classes and a whole lunch period without any issues. And I got to sit next to Suzie in algebra! By the time I headed for my last two classes of the day, I thought maybe, just maybe, there was an upside to the divorce, the two homes, the change of schools, the whole life ruined for ever thing.

"Mr Pickings," said Mrs Bowers in an exasperated manner that made me realise she'd been saying my name repeatedly. Why do teachers always think using your last name will make them sound more intimidating? It never does, especially in the raspy monotone Mrs Bowers uses that makes her seem so bored even her glasses lose the will to stay on her nose. Upon hearing my last name, the whole class snickered. And I felt the cold shudder of familiar insecurities running up my spine. The same thing happened at my last school. Otis Miller would hide behind his book to my right, stick his finger up his nose, and pretend to flick boogers at me while whispering, "Picky Pickings," as if it were actually clever.

I had been so relieved when his family moved across town and he got transferred out of my school. But one disgusting sniffle behind me was all it took to remind me where he had been transferred to.

Like a slow-motion reveal in a horror movie, I turned round to see Otis Miller and his lanky limbs folded into a desk right behind me. "Picky Pickings!" he said with a wicked smile and a finger up his nose.

I instantly felt a rush of blood heating my cheeks as I turned to face the front. "Mr Pickings," continued Mrs Bowers, "since you missed homeroom this morning, would you please stand up and introduce yourself now? Tell us something we should know about you." I should have seen it coming. Despite multiple periods of glorious anonymity, there was no way to make it through an entire first day at a new school without some sadistic teacher torturing me with unnecessary personal introductions.

My legs wobbled as I forced myself to stand. Everyone was staring at me. Dismissive. Expectant. Judgemental. A paper crumpled. Another loud, gross sniffle from Otis followed. Then whispers. And snickers. And a couple of subdued laughs. I was frozen. Tunnel vision set in and the room felt uneven. I didn't want anyone to know anything about me. That was the whole point of today. I wanted to be no one. I wanted to not exist. But I couldn't and I did. I had to at least say my name. Just as I managed to prise my dry mouth open, something hit me. Literally. A wet, sticky glob was stuck to the back of my neck.

I spun and saw that Otis looked almost as shocked as I did that he'd actually flung his actual booger and that it was actually stuck to my actual neck. He clearly didn't mean to take it that far and I didn't know how to respond now that he did. Normally his disgusting sniffling was enough to get under my skin. But this time, his booger-snot was *on* my skin.

I wiped it with my hand, but then it got stuck there and I tried to flick it back at him, but it just got stuck to my finger instead. Mrs Bowers was yelling something unintelligible. In my panic, I started to flail around like I was trying to get away from my own hand. I felt a full-blown panic attack coming on. Who knows what noxious germs are in Otis Miller's boogers?! So, I did the only thing I could think to do: I wiped it on Heather Hu. She was sitting in front of me and I thought it would come right off on her perfectly curated hair.

I'm not exactly sure what happened after that. There was a lot of squealing and stampeding. I heard more than one person yell "Booger!" But I was paralysed with panic on the cold, cracked floor tiles. There were a lot of squeaking shoes and crashing chairs, a lot of screams and shouts that all melded together into one overwhelming *ROAR*. I clenched my eyes tight, but when I opened them again, the whole class was blurry. They were one giant, roaring MONSTER. I curled up into the smallest ball I could be, willing myself to be anywhere but there.

Next thing I knew, I got my wish. Mrs Bowers was dragging me by the ear to the principal's office. The panic had faded enough that I could sort of breathe again. "You've made quite a first impression, Mr Pickings," she proclaimed, as if I somehow started this. "And it's not a good one."

"He flicked a booger at me. What did you want me to do?" I asked, as if there couldn't possibly be a more rational response to a wet booger hitting my neck than a total and utter meltdown.

"Get a tissue," was her exhausted response, punctuated by shoving her glasses back onto her nose and slamming the office door behind me.

I took a seat in the lumpy chair I had started the day

in and tried to calm down as I waited for the familiar soft shuffle of Nurse Nellie's feet coming down the hallway to deliver a child-size Xanax. But then I remembered – Nurse Nellie is in my old school and I'm on a medication vacation. I don't even know if my parents told this school about my issues or gave them my emergency prescription. They haven't been on top of things lately. And there wasn't even a receptionist at the front desk at the moment. The principal's door was closed. And I was left sitting there all alone.

Just me and my thoughts.

I thought of Suzie, thankful that she wasn't in that class to witness my meltdown. But then I realised that she knows everyone and will totally hear about it anyway. Some of the kids probably even caught it on their phones. *I'll be a meme before the last bell,* I thought. *It will almost certainly haunt my existence right into high school. I'll be known for ever as "Picky Pickings" and taunted for sport!*

My heart was racing. My thoughts were totally spiralling away from me. A therapist once tried to teach me how to reframe my thoughts while deep breathing, but I had my own unique take on that exercise. I slumped over in my own lap, squeezing my head between my knees, inhaling and exhaling and trying to focus. Trying to regain control of my own brain.

A thought spiral. One push down that slippery slope and my brain will just spin faster and faster until I feel totally out of control. I'm getting better at slowing myself down now, but back then, I thought it would never end. It was like falling into a bottomless pit. I was a mess. I was furious. I was mortified. I was really sad. I had a chance to be normal – or at least to seem normal – and I'd blown it. I'd totally blown it. It took less than a day for my new life in my new school to become just like my old life in my old school.

At some point, a grumpy, wrinkled receptionist who smelled of butterscotch and air freshener came back from the copy room and found me slouched down and dejected. "The new kid is back already," she announced to Principal Waters, who opened his door, smoothed out his jarringly plaid trousers, straightened his jarringly plaid matching tie, and took me into his office to give me a pep talk about fresh starts and adjusting to a new school and giving myself a chance.

But I had zoned out and couldn't focus on anything he said. I had entered my standard post-panic recovery period. I felt numb and couldn't manage much more than to nod and mumble back a perfunctory "Yes," and

"Okay," and "I will." I've learned that adults need to feel like they're being heard even when they have no idea what they're talking about. It makes them feel good and it earns you some peace and quiet a lot faster.

"I've seen your file and I just don't want you to have the same problems you had in your previous school, Steven," said Principal Waters, leaning forward on his desk. "Do you prefer Steven or Steve? Or even Stevie? I've always liked Stevie. But I'm a big fan of Fleetwood Mac."

I had no idea what he was talking about, but he clearly expected an answer, so I opened my mouth and told him way more than anyone needs to know: "My family used to call me Stevie because it's cute to do that when you're a little blob of nothing and no one takes you seriously. But eventually I formed a personality and I guess it wasn't cute any more. So, they started calling me Slim – as in 'Slim Pickings'. I think they meant it as a term of endearment, but I think they also thought it was funny. It doesn't bother me, except when it does. But I'm easily bothered. And I don't know, I guess if you were looking for something that wouldn't bother me, it would be slim pickings, so they call me Slim Pickings. It's really not even that clever. But it's my name now – so I guess you can call me that too."

And Principal Waters stared at me slack-jawed for a moment. Like a lot of people I try to talk to, he had no idea how to respond to me. I think we were both happy that my dad burst in at that moment. "Hey, Slim," he said with an air of wariness and disappointment I've grown accustomed to. He had on a suit, so I knew he must have been on his way to (or pulled out of) an important meeting.

He'd barely introduced himself to the principal when my mom rushed in, all frantic and full of questions. "Slim? What happened? What's the problem? What . . . are *you* doing here?!" She skidded to a stop when she realised Dad was already here. "Dale, it's my day," she continued as she pulled out her phone to double-check her schedule. Mom is the queen of checklists and schedules, even though she's been all over the place lately.

Dad rubbed the stress stubble that seems to have become a permanent fixture on his face and replied, "Does it matter any more? I got pulled out of work for this."

Mom couldn't help but correct him: "We both did."

Principal Waters sent me back outside to the lumpy chair and shut the door. I couldn't hear what they were saying but I could see Mom and Dad having a serious conversation with him through his frosted window. It actually looked a lot more like couples therapy than anything else, and it was making me feel anxious again. So when the grumpy receptionist wasn't looking, I slipped outside so I could breathe.

That worked – for about thirty seconds.

"Way to go, Booger Boy," said Lucy as she walked up to me and shoved her phone in my face. My life literally flashed before my eyes. Or the most recent episode did. My meltdown had, in fact, gone viral before the last bell. "My new friend Maya sent this to me," she explained. "Luckily it was *after* she introduced me to the whole soccer team and I got invited to their sleepover this weekend. Otherwise it would be super embarrassing for me," she added. Because of course she had already made new friends.

Lucy's technically my little sister, but it's weird to call her "little" since she's almost as tall as I am. "Younger" is more accurate. She's only ten, but according to that horribly awkward sex education class in my old school where sweaty Mr Felcher stuttered his way through a lesson on puberty, boys hit their growth spurts later than girls.

Most comparisons between us tend to fall in her favour. Lucy's strong where I'm scrawny, she's focused where I'm distracted, and she has an effortless sort of poise about her while I have an effortless sort of dork about me. To paraphrase Dad when he didn't know I was listening, "She's got her poop together." Except he didn't say "poop".

BRRRRING! The last bell rang and kids were purged from the school like vomit, which is what I felt like, considering everyone was still laughing at me. "Hey, Bestie!" shrieked a girl I quickly deduced was Lucy's new best friend, Maya Rodriguez, which seemed impossible since they just met today. Maya raved on and on, "I love your jeans, and your bag, and you have to send me a link to those cleats you got so we can all get the same ones for the team. The sleepover this weekend will be so much fun!" As if I needed a reminder that Lucy did not have the same problems as me.

"One day and you're already insta-famous." I turned to see Suzie laughing at my video, and cringed out of deathly embarrassment. "Don't worry, Slim," she told me in that soothing voice of hers. "Last year I went viral after sitting on a chocolate pudding cup in white trousers. I was 'Suzie Skidmark' for weeks. But the news cycle moved on. Your fifteen minutes of fame will be over fast."

And that's when I realised she actually wasn't laughing at me. She was just smiling at me. Like I wasn't a total freak. She pulled out one of those organic, vegan, gluten-free, dairy-free, nut-free, sugar-free, all-natural snack bars and took a bite like everything was totally cool and completely normal. I didn't know what to say but I desperately wanted to say something so that she'd stick around. My mouth made words that sounded like, "IS THAT GOOD?"

I kind of shouted it really loud and fast and probably turned bright red. "I, um . . . I like snack bars too," was my totally smooth follow-up. My mind spun like a buffering laptop as I registered her signature scent. When I snapped out of it, I realised she was in the middle of telling me, ". . . and they're made with whole, natural ingredients, which my dads say are much better than all those chemically processed snacks. They're thinking of selling them in the wellness centre, which means I could eat as many as I want! Not that I would because it's all about balance, right?"

I think I nodded my head. "I only like all-natural ingredients. I really, really hate any chemically processed products!" I said-shouted. I didn't care that I didn't even know what I was talking about. I was talking to a girl. And not just any girl – Suzie Minkle with those bright eyes and a smile that maybe I helped put there.

"Ha!" My sister laughed loud enough for Suzie to hear. "Xanax, Ritalin, Zoloft, Lexapro," she said, naming the entire alien galaxy of chemical wonder-drugs I've ingested over the past couple of years. "Not to mention the Twizzlers I know you have stashed in your room. That's like straight high-fructose corn syrup," she added.

Suzie's smile faded a bit, but didn't disappear. "You don't have to pretend to be into the things that I'm into. I like Twizzlers too," she said. But then Suzie spotted her bus and ran towards it, shouting, "See you tomorrow!" And just like that, the really nice smell was gone too.

I was left alone with Lucy and her smug-satisfied grin.

Mom and Dad came outside, which reminded me that at least I'd be spared the indignity of the bus ride home. I could see that they'd agreed to try to get along for a minute and to focus on me. They had that "we're sorry" look on their faces, like somehow my freak-out was all their fault. "How are you feeling, Slim? Any withdrawal symptoms?" asked Mom in that mom-way they must teach at the hospital before they let new parents bring a baby home. "Any brain shivers? Or are they zaps? It just sounds awful either way."

Luckily I wasn't feeling them this time around. "So far this medication vacation is a first-class getaway. I'm especially enjoying the bottomless margaritas and long walks on the beach," was the totally sarcastic response my brain formulated, but my mouth could only spit out, "I'm fine."

"Your episode in class suggests otherwise," corrected Dad.

He was right. Everything was lousy right now, but not because my brain was revolting from a lack of prescription drugs.

"Are you good now? Do you need a Xanax?" asked Mom, rifling through her bag to no avail. "Oh, I must have left them at the site."

Dad scoffed. "The 'site,' Leslie? Really? You mean our house?"

Mom sighed. "Yes. Our house. Except it's not ours any more. We sold it. And the new owners hired me to renovate it. That's my job, Dale. That's how I provide for our kids."

"And I don't?"

"That's not what I said."

"It's what you implied."

"Look, I just need to know if you can take them now or not? It won't be safe for them to hang out at the site . . . *the old house* . . . with the fumigation crew."

The fact that they were fumigating only after we moved out didn't seem fair. Why was it okay for us to live with pests but not some strangers? But then again, maybe that was the point. Maybe our pest-filled life needed to be aired out of the house before the next family could move in. Hopefully, they'd have better luck in it than we did. Or maybe they'd end up just like us. Who knows? Who cares?

Lucy and I slipped into Dad's Jeep to get away from the bickering, and as she shut the door she couldn't help but tell me, "You've taken so many pills, it's no wonder you've become one yourself." I was tempted to argue, but I knew she had a point. I'd been on five different medications since that first episode. A couple of them helped for a little while, but they all had different effects — and side effects. Some gave me headaches, some dry skin, some left me unable to sleep, and one even made my symptoms a little worse. Go figure. The doctors always said it would be a process of trial and error, but really it felt more like a trail of errors.

"Fine, I'll call the therapist," Dad told Mom as he climbed into the front seat. "I'll fix everything," he muttered to himself as he slammed the car door shut.

After they broke up this past summer, Dad spent a month in a motel before he moved into a "temporary" two-bedroom apartment. He furnished it with his half of our old life. For whatever reason, he got the old bedroom dresser, the living-room sofa, and a coffee table that we'd kept in the basement. Mom got all the lamps. Why? I have no idea. And the fact that Dad's apartment had only two bedrooms meant Lucy and I had to share a room when we stayed with him, which I'm pretty sure qualifies as cruel and unusual punishment.

Things were a little better on Mom's end, where she had us set up in a new model home in the housing development she's been putting together in a swankier part of Old Wayford. As if anywhere in Connecticut needs new housing developments – especially ones where all the houses look exactly the same. It was really nice and much roomier than Dad's apartment, but it didn't feel like home. Except for a few of the lamps, Mom kept nothing from the old place. And potential new buyers were coming through all the time, so we could barely put anything up to make it look like we even lived there. At that point, I felt like just another decorative design accessory. And I couldn't help but wonder if things would have been different if I had been less of a problem the past two years.

"This is never going to work," I said out loud, but mostly to myself.

"Great. So then it will be just like it was before," added Lucy.

Outside, the buses were pulling away and Mom forced a smile and waved goodbye to us in that way parents smile when they think they're somehow fooling you that everything is totally fine. I should know. I've perfected that face myself.

Dad shifted the car into gear and flipped on the radio. "Just in time for rush-hour traffic. I'm gonna be late for my focus group," he said. "So now you get to come to work with me, which will be super fun for everyone!"

His sarcasm was met with silence. If by "super fun" he meant feeling like a lab rat in a poorly designed experiment called "life", then he was totally on point. I just wish I knew then how literal that comparison was about to become.

I used to think that mad science only happens in movies.

But then I went to Clarity Labs.

CHAPTER 2

THE EXPOSURE

Clarity Labs was a sprawling building. All cold, clinical, clean lines and sanitised spaces. Imagine an Apple store crossed with a crime show morgue on serious steroids. Everything was shiny. Everything was either metal or glass. And every section seemed to be on lockdown. Dad had to swipe us in with his security card every time we turned a corner. Everyone who worked there seemed to have one of two modes: forced smiles or serious scowls. Both options made me uneasy. I trailed after Lucy, who rushed after Dad down the echo chamber hallways until he suddenly disappeared into a conference room without us. The door shut with a *CLICK* behind him, leaving me and Lucy to wonder what the heck just happened.

Dad must have realised this a moment later when he popped his head back out, pointing at an uncomfortable-looking metal bench. "Wait here. Do your homework. And keep an eye on her," he said, motioning to my totally annoyed sister as if I had any control over what she does. It might have been an honest mistake, but at least this time, I was nominally in charge. Usually it worked the other way, since I was the mess and she was the one who had her poop together.

We slumped onto the bench in the hall, which was exactly as cold and uncomfortable as it looked. For a moment, I could hear Dad talking to whoever was inside that room. "Hello, and welcome to Clarity Labs. I'm Dale Pickings, Vice President of Marketing, and I'm excited to talk to you today about Personal Vex—" Until, *CLICK*, the door shut and locked again.

In an attempt to fulfil my duties as a responsible older brother, I pulled out my algebra homework and tried to do as I was told. But Lucy immediately started playing Candy Crush on her phone at full volume. Every chirp, chime and musical victory was amplified by the metal sound chamber we were trapped in. "Could you hit the mute button, please?" I asked as nicely as I could manage despite the candy-coloured music sending my nerves into overdrive.

This was met with a scoff from Lucy and the telltale celebratory music of a level-up. "Seriously, don't you have homework to do?" I asked, attempting to control the annoyance in my voice.

She just smirked and rolled her eyes and said, "That's what study hall is for." I tried to focus on my homework again, but her Candy Crush was crushing my concentration. I could tell from the stupid smile on Lucy's face that her goal was no longer to level-up in the game, but just to level-up my irritation. I hated that it was working, but I was determined to not let her win.

I slammed my book shut and closed my eyes. I leaned back against the wall behind me and did . . . nothing. The thing about Lucy is that she wants attention. And I knew the best way to annoy her was to totally ignore her.

And it worked. Lucy shifted so she was facing me, hoping the game noise would make me react. And although I was screaming on the inside, I refused to let her get a rise out of me. This was the sort of standoff we had at least once a day. I usually lost because . . . well, because I'm me. But this time I was distracted because I realised if I concentrated, I could hear Dad through the wall. "Clarity Labs is now refocusing our brand to appeal to the parents of the modern Millennial market. Chemicals are out of favour and natural remedies are trending." I hadn't heard him say that before. It made me think of Suzie. I pressed my ear to the wall.

But now that I wasn't actively agitated by her game,

Lucy was getting restless. She tends to do that when no one is paying attention to her. When Dad stopped talking, I opened my eyes again – and Lucy was gone. It had only been a minute, but she'd lost her patience and taken off down the hall. The only thing that kept me calm was the fact that you can't get anywhere in this building without a security card. She couldn't actually leave this hallway.

So I was stunned when I saw her swipe a card at the security pad beside the first set of doors. She paused for a moment to flip me off before disappearing. She must have stolen Dad's security card! This wasn't the first time she'd taken something (or "borrowed", as she puts it) without asking. It'd been happening more and more since we moved. If something was missing, I knew who took it, and I knew it would take for ever to get it back. I gave up asking a long time ago. Usually I would just ransack her room to find it. But this was a whole new level of "borrowing". This could get us both in real trouble.

I knew I had to act quickly if I didn't want Dad to find out. I looked around for help, but there was no one in the hall. My leg was shaking and my nerves were frayed and I just couldn't be alone. Without thinking, I launched myself at the door before it shut.

The door closed behind me with an audible *CLICK* that echoed down the halls of the actual labs of Clarity Labs like a warning. I was suddenly terrified that I would get caught. I had zero excuses ready. No one would buy that I just got lost. And I started to worry what sort of punishment would be handed out to underage trespassers. One side of the hallway was lined with heavy metal doors with little glass windows in them. The other side was broken up by glass-walled rooms where lab technicians went about their business on all sorts of sophisticated equipment. Even though no one seemed to notice (or care) that I was there, I crouched down out of sight anyway. I crept down the hall as slowly and soundlessly as possible until I was right under a sign reading, "Authorised Personnel Only Beyond This Point". The big, bold, red and black letters were so aggressive I was afraid to step past it. Instead, I leaned forward and whispered urgently, "Lucy?!" Her name bounced down the echo chamber of a hallway, but I didn't hear a response. Annoyed, I took a deep breath and stepped forward, breaking the invisible line where it was okay to be authorised or not, knowing full well this was a bad idea – an awful idea, actually – but also knowing, too, a far worse idea would be letting

Lucy get in trouble the only time Dad ever told me to keep an eye on her.

But then a *click-clacking* of heels coming closer stopped me dead in my tracks. With the echoes, I couldn't tell if it was coming from ahead of me or from behind. I didn't know what to do or where to go. *Click-clack, click-clack.* A closet. I spied a closet. I rattled the handle, but it *buzzed* to let me know it would remain locked without a security card. *Click-clack, click-clack.* I backed up into a nearby doorframe and froze. Trying to be invisible, but fully knowing I was so about to be busted.

And then . . . just when I was sure I was about to be headed to jail or reform school, a hand reached out and grabbed me and yanked me into the room on the other side of the door. I nearly screamed but Lucy clamped a hand over my mouth and gently closed the door until it was open just a crack so she could keep an eye out.

We both listened as the *click-clacking* came closer, and I peeked over her shoulder as a power-suited executive and an older man in a rumpled white lab coat came into view. "Ms Salt . . . Ms Salt, a moment please!" I'd later find out that this was Dr Hugo Zanker, the lead research scientist at Clarity Labs. He was an unpredictable man with perpetually bloodshot eyes and a twitchy demeanour. "We need to start human trials!" he said with a desperate gleam in his eye.

The power suit turned sharply. It was Pauline Salt, CEO of Clarity Labs. I recognised her from her portrait in the front lobby. Her dark, angular face contrasted sharply with a pristinely tailored suit that was the same colour as her last name. "Dr Zanker, the future of Clarity Labs depends on me to make all the right decisions at all the right times. If we rush towards human trials, the FDA might start questioning the origin of Project PVZ."

"But the rats are inconclusive," Dr Zanker pleaded. "How will I know if I've made the proper alterations to the formula without human—"

Ms Salt silenced him with a finger. Zanker was desperate to argue, but Ms Salt was having none of it. Everything about her just screamed, *This discussion is over*. But instead, she didn't even have to raise her voice. She just straightened her suit and spoke with the authority of a press release. "PVZ is an 'all-natural' anti-anxiety treatment intended to temporarily absorb and dispose of irritations to create calmer, consistent consumers for Clarity Labs. One purpose. One formula. No previous version. End of product description."

"But . . ." continued Dr Zanker, to no avail.

"Plausible deniability is our friend, Dr Zanker," said Pauline Salt, just before she leaned forward and added in a conspiratorial tone, "You and I both know that if the FDA starts poking around, we won't survive Plum Island."

Pauline Salt then turned and *click-clacked* away while Dr Zanker shuffled back the way they had come, arguing with himself as he went.

Lucy let the door click shut and we both exhaled a sigh of relief.

"You're gonna get us in so much trouble," I said. "We *really* shouldn't be here." I grabbed for her arm, thinking we'd sneak our way back to the safety of that horrible metal bench. But she dodged and turned to explore the room we'd wandered into.

"No one made you come after me."

"No one made you . . . be stupid," was the best my frazzled brain could offer. She looked at me like "good one" and kept going. I didn't know what else to do but follow her.

The room was filled with dozens of cages that housed dozens of lab rats. In front of each cage hung different digital readings and handwritten charts.

"Animal testing is so messed up," she spun round to

tell me. "If Dad wouldn't lose his job, I'd totally set them all free right now."

"I don't know. The little guys look okay to me." And they did. No visible wounds. No extra limbs. No unidentifiable growths.

"Whoa, what's up with this one?" she said, pointing at one of the rats. It was freaking out. Shaking and squeaking and scurrying around in its cage like it was bothered by something that wasn't there.

We peered in and looked more closely at the rat. At first I thought that maybe it was just a little hyper, but then it started to seem like it was swatting at the air, like there was a bug in the cage that no one could see. Lucy stepped back and looked at the rest of the rats, suddenly realising . . . "A lot of them are acting that way."

And she was right. About half the rats in the place looked like they were going crazy.

I picked up the handwritten chart hanging off the first rat's cage. "Personal Vexation Zoners. PVZ." Then I looked up at Lucy. "PVZ is what they were just talking about in the hall!" I dropped the chart and backed away. "Oh, this can't be good. We really need to get out of here."

"Stop freaking out, Slim. You didn't have to follow

me. If you're so eager to get out of here," Lucy said as she shoved me towards the door, "then get out!"

And I tried to resist, but something in her just cracked. She pushed and pushed and pushed until she yanked the door open and pushed me out the same way she'd just pulled me in. I tumbled out into the hallway and crashed right into Dr Zanker. I remember everything as if it all happened in super slo-mo. Dr Zanker wasn't watching where he was going. He was in a hurry and certainly didn't expect a kid to crash into him in the middle of the hallway. He was wearing a surgical mask and carrying a small nasal spray bottle. I slammed into him in mid-stride, knocking the bottle out of his hands. He fumbled for it, but he only slapped it up into the air even higher. I fell in a flop to the floor, and a moment later, the bottle hit the cold, hard tiles too. Right in front of me. Close enough that I could read the label – Personal Vexation Zoners (PVZ). Close enough that when it cracked open I got a big whiff of it right in the face.

I immediately panicked. Instead of covering my mouth, I gasped for air. Not smart. By the time I sat up, the PVZ bottle was empty and I'd inhaled it all.

"What did you just do!" shouted Dr Zanker as he snatched up the broken bottle.

I leaped to my feet and wiped my face as if that would somehow get rid of the evidence. I wasn't sure what to do. I was about to take off, make a run for it, when a fire alarm rang out. The hall quickly flooded with lab technicians and employees. As Dr Zanker scrambled to collect the broken pieces of his PVZ bottle, Lucy came out of nowhere, grabbed my arm, and ushered me into the crowd.

Before I could really process what had happened, we'd gone back through the main door between the labs we should never have gone into in the first place and the hallway we should have been waiting in this whole time. Up ahead, Dad guided his focus group towards the lobby. "Just remain calm," he said, "like PVZ will make you. Eventually. When it's approved for mass consumption." One of the focus group members gave him a dirty glare, so he shouted to the whole group, "And don't worry, you'll still get your free vouchers!"

I headed towards him, but Lucy stopped me before he could see where we had come from. We saw Dad look at the empty bench, realise we weren't there, and then spin around to scan for us. Lucy pushed us behind a rather large lab tech, and by the time Dad had done a full 360, we were back sitting on the bench as if we'd never left.

"Oh, where . . . I just . . ." Dad stammered, confused.

"Never mind. We need to evacuate." As he guided us both towards the lobby, I saw Lucy slip his security card back in his pocket. She was so much sneakier than I ever imagined. The fire alarm kept blaring and that's when I put it together.

"Did you pull—" But I was cut off by Lucy's elbow in my rib cage. Dad took one look at me and asked his standard, "Hey, are you okay?" He saw me look accusingly at Lucy and asked the even more standard, "What's going on?"

I don't exactly know how to explain it, but despite how much we drive each other crazy, we must have some instinctive sibling bond that sparks in times of crisis. Without even hesitating, we both said, "Nothing!" as if it had to be the truth. Dad wasn't convinced, but there was no time for cross-examinations. We had just made it to the lobby exit when Pauline Salt popped up out of nowhere, like a jump scare in a horror movie. "The focus group was cut short, Dale. This whole day is now void," she said, completely oblivious to the concerned people trying to get to safety all around her. "You'll have to redo it. We go to the board next week. No mistakes. No excuses."

Dad stared at her like a chastised child. "But . . . it's a fire alarm."

"No. Excuses," she reiterated. And then Pauline Salt *click-clacked* away, against the tide of the crowd, back towards the labs as if the fire better be afraid of *her*.

As I watched her go, I spotted Dr Zanker frantically searching the crowd. We made eye contact, and he lit up like I was the dessert tray after a fancy meal. "Slim!" Dad shouted after me, reminding me that I was once again two steps behind them. I ran to catch up, slipping through the door just as it was shutting. The last thing I saw through the closing gap was Dr Zanker standing there, still watching me, as a creepy, giddy smile slid across his face.

We parked in the driveway of the model home after a long ride in total silence. Dad seemed to be preoccupied with work. And considering how Pauline Salt had chewed him out, I didn't blame him. Lucy kept quiet in the back seat, not even using her phone. I was pretty sure she was just trying to keep a low profile to prevent me from abruptly ratting her out about sneaking into the labs.

But any hope of remaining calm and quiet was shot when I went inside. Mom took one look at me and rained down questions I didn't have the energy to answer: "Are you okay? You look pale. Are you sick?

What did Dad do with you? Did he give you candy? Is it a tummy ache? You know sugar doesn't help your anxiety. Did you at least do your homework? Why are you looking at me like that? What happened?"

Thankfully, Dad was totally in the mood to answer that last question. "What happened, Leslie, is that you screwed up our schedules – AGAIN."

Lucy had already run upstairs to avoid getting roped into the drama. But I couldn't pull myself away. It was like watching a car crash you're powerless to stop.

"I didn't 'screw up' our schedules, Dale; you just never bother to listen to anyone."

Dad scoffed. "Oh, I hear you. Trying to control everything and everyone as usual." And from there came a familiar litany of complaints – the missed opportunities, the forgotten anniversaries, the lack of empathy, the time we got stuck at that gas station on the way to Big Moose Lake. (Dad locked the keys inside the car!) I knew exactly how the rest would go and that it wouldn't stop until one of them said something mean enough to end it. I didn't need to stick around to witness that part. So, I trudged up the stairs after Lucy and shut the door to my model room in my model home right above my not-so-model parents, who I could still hear shouting.

"Fire alarm?! After what Slim already went through today? Did you WANT him to have another episode?"

"Slim was fine! He *is* fine! Well, mostly. And anyway, my focus group today was for a new treatment that could end up helping him when it's released."

"Oh God, you sound just like that sociopathic boss of yours," Mom shot back. "We agreed to this 'medication vacation'," she continued. "And I'm looking for a new therapist, since he won't actually talk to the one we're wasting money on. I just haven't found the—"

"TIME?" Dad scoffed again. "All those years and God forbid I missed one of your imaginary deadlines for mowing the lawn or replacing the Brita filter, but you can't hit a deadline on helping our son?"

No matter what the fight started about, it always included what to do about me.

I always seemed to be the problem.

I lifted the bottom edges of a life-size Spider-Man poster (one of the few personal touches I was allowed to add to our model life), revealing an almost unnoticeable little door in the wall. It was built to be a storage cubby, but it's got a little light inside and over the past few weeks, I'd filled it with blankets and comics and a good-size candy stash. It's my "safe space". No one knew about it. I crawled in, shut the door, put a pillow over my face, and screamed my frustrations into it. When I was done, I felt a little better. I opened an X-Men comic, grabbed some Twizzlers, and gnawed down three at a time until my parents' shouting faded away and I heard Dad slam the door and leave.

Everything got very still and very quiet after that. I almost felt like I could breathe again, but as soon as I realised that, I began to feel guilty. Like I was happy my parents weren't together. And that's how I would feel if it really were my fault. I got a sinking feeling in my gut, and it wasn't from the candy. My thought spiral was picking up speed again, so I started doing the mental exercises my therapist gave me to reframe my negative thoughts. I told myself that I'm okay. That everything is going to be okay. Then I got specific. I remembered Pauline Salt saying PVZ is for anxiety issues. So I thought to myself, *Maybe I'm starting to calm down because the PVZ is actually working.* It was a long shot, but I doubled down on it with, *Maybe I'll go to bed tonight and wake up tomorrow and be cured of whatever is really wrong with me.* And then I glanced at the mutant heroes in the glossy pages of my comic book and really went for it with the ridiculous, *Or maybe I'll even wake up and discover this exposure to PVZ has given me some sort of superpower!* A moment later, reality set in and I started to worry about the far more likely scenario that the PVZ would give me hives or brain zaps or make me grow hair on my eyeballs.

It turned out I wasn't totally wrong. It did give me something. Or some things, to be precise. But they definitely weren't superpowers. And they definitely weren't a cure.

CHAPTER 3

THE AWAKENING

The sound was the worst. Every morning. The *BEEP BEEP BEEP BEEP* of my alarm clock ruined my day before I was even awake. Every morning I'd rip my eyes open, annoyed, and swear to destroy it. And every morning I'd totally lose the energy to do so as soon as it was off.

That morning was no different. *BEEP BEEP BEEP BEEP*. I shot up in bed and swatted the clock, silencing it by knocking it onto the floor. Then I sneezed really hard – a giant "ACHOO!" that blew my head back onto the pillow, where I was determined to grab a few more minutes of shut-eye anyway.

But before I could even get comfortable, it started again – *BEEP BEEP BEEP BEEP*. Without opening my eyes, I lunged for the clock, falling halfway off my bed in the process. I managed to find it and hit the snooze button – but nothing happened. Really annoyed now, I yanked the power cord out, but still, somehow, the *BEEP BEEP BEEP BEEP* kept going. Confused, I gave up on sleeping more and opened my eyes instead.

And there it was. I didn't know WHAT it was. But it was there at the foot of my bed – a furry little potato sack with two arms, beady little eyes and massive ears that twitched around like satellite dishes. Its big, gaping, froglike mouth was spewing out this horrendous sound – *BEEP BEEP BEEP BEEP*.

I fell out of bed, hitting my head on my nightstand when I tried to scramble away. I rubbed the sleep out of my eyes, desperate for this to be a bad dream, but the little purple creature just sat there, looking up at me with innocent eyes, almost smiling as it rhythmically droned on *BEEP BEEP BEEP BEEP*. It was awful. I covered my ears, but the little creature seemed pleased that I did that. As if it had accomplished a goal.

I jumped back up on my bed, grabbed the pillows closest to me, and threw them at it as hard as I could. But the creature seemed oblivious. It hopped up on my desk, happy as can be, and began to explore what seemed like a whole new world. It walked over my keyboard. *CLICK CLICK CLICK CLICK*. It paused and stomped again. *CLICK*. It smiled.

CLICK CLICK CLICK CLICK came out of its mouth as "WHAT THE HELL ARE YOU?!" came out of mine. It hopped off the desk and approached the foot of my bed. I panicked and scrambled across the bed to grab my Wolverine gloves off a shelf. *SNIKT!* The plastic claws popped out with the pre-programmed sound effect.

SNIKT! SNIKT! SNIKT! SNIKT! the creature said, hopping up on my bed as if I'd asked it to follow me. I jumped off the other side, swiping my claws at it, but it just kept coming closer, seemingly excited by the sound of it alone. My foot got tangled in the dirty laundry on the floor and I fell with a *THUD.*

THUD THUD THUD THUD it said, smiling, as it stepped closer.

"Get back. Get away. STAY AWAY!" I shouted, swatting the air in its general direction.

THUD THUD THUD THUD. It was almost on me. I clenched up and did the only reasonable thing left.

"MOM!" I yelled. What else was I supposed to do?

She came rushing into the room. "What is all the racket up . . ." and then she stopped short, her eyes wide in horror at what she saw. "I don't believe this," she said, stomping in like she was ready to take charge and shut the creature up. "Slim, I've told you a hundred times that the floor is not a laundry basket." And she walked right past the noisy, potato-sack-looking creature and picked up the clothes I had just tripped over.

I must have been in shock because I couldn't really form another word. I just pointed with a confused and freaked-out look on my face. In response, the creature opened its mouth. *BEEP BEEP BEEP BEEP.* "We need to keep this place neat for clients so I can actually afford these clothes you toss on the floor," she continued, talking right over the noise as if she couldn't hear anything.

She must have seen the colour drain from my face because she sat me down on the edge of my bed and felt my forehead. "Honey, you look pale. Are you sick? You're sweating. Do you have chills? It's not a fever. Did you sleep okay?" Mom never seemed to run out of things to ask me, even though I never have enough answers for her. Especially while staring at an incredibly loud and furry monster that seemed to not exist to her at all. "I really hope you aren't coming down with something," she continued. "Is this about yesterday? Are you still worked up over it? Or are you just angling for a mental health day here?" I didn't feel sick, but I did feel super annoyed at the onslaught of questions when the only relevant question anyone should be asking was, "WHAT THE HELL IS

THAT?!" And then, without warning, I sneezed again.

"Maybe it's just allergies. Do you think it's allergies? You don't usually have allergies, but sometimes they develop," she pointed out. And as she kept talking, I saw something else develop.

My sneeze had taken me by surprise, so I didn't have time to cover it up. And right on the floor where it had sprayed, I saw the tiny, clear drops start to pull together into a translucent glob of goo, almost like a booger . . . but bigger . . . and it moved! It stretched and expanded and started to form a mosslike film on its surface that quickly turned into a bluish fur. Then a pair of eyes popped through, looking all around like it was fascinated at everything it saw.

"Slim, honey, just breathe. You don't want a panic attack now," Mom said, attempting to calm me down. "Remember what your therapist said about breathing through it?" I nodded, trying to breathe, hoping she was right. But I couldn't take my eyes off the new little monster.

The fur ball with eyes rocked back and forth until *POP* – a pair of arms sprang from its sides, and it pressed its paws against the floor and pushed itself up, stretching its potato-sack body until it was standing on two little feet. It rubbed its head until a pair of pointy ears flicked out. And now this second furry little creature was looking up at me with the biggest, most curious eyes I'd ever seen – like it wanted to know all it could about every single thing it saw. A few crooked little teeth jutted out from its head as its furry face formed a mouth. When it opened, I was expecting another round of beeping noises, but that's not what this one did at all; instead, it asked, "Am I an allergy?"

That was enough to send me skittering off the bed and on top of the noisy creature on the other side. I could feel it squish below me, like a deflating air mattress. It was a weird, unpleasant sensation, and when I rolled off, the noisy thing was flattened on the floor. I crab-crawled away as far as I could get from the creatures I had somehow sneezed into existence. As I tried to gain control of my breathing, the flattened one re-formed, seemingly unharmed, and started beeping again. I tried to get away but I was pinned against my dresser. My one-thousand-and-forty-seven piece Lego Batman set that took me three days to assemble fell off the top and shattered on the floor. I'd never get it back together again. Mom had thrown out the directions in the move. I wanted to scream. The noisy one's satellite-like ears twitched in my direction. *CRASH CRASH CRASH CRASH* it repeated like my Lego masterpiece would never stop breaking, while the other creature picked up my scattered Lego pieces, asking rapid-fire, "What are these? Why did you do that? Where are you going?"

I backed away from the mess and over towards Mom, who was visibly frustrated by my freak-out. "Slim, for heaven's sake, what are you so upset about?" she asked.

"You don't see them?!" I shouted.

She looked around and her eyes finally landed on the creatures. "Oh, I sure do," she said. She walked right over to the creatures this time, bent down between them, and picked up some candy wrappers I forgot to hide. "Did you eat these before bed? What did you expect with all that sugar in your system? And what have I told you about leaving food in your room? It attracts pests! This is why I had to have the old house fumigated for the new owners!" she lectured, while the second little creature looked up at me and asked, "Am I a pest? Is she blind? Are you crazy?"

I looked back at Mom as she got to her classic, "I'm not a maid service, Slim." Lucy popped her head in the room to check out the commotion. I had never been so happy to see her. Surely, she'd be able to see these little creatures and prove I wasn't losing my mind.

But Lucy just looked at the mess and said, "He actually has a whole candy stash hidden in here." She's such a tattletale. Normally I would have snapped at her, but instead I sneezed.

"Lucy, go and get ready for school," said Mom. Lucy stomped off down the hall as another voice entered the fray.

I turned in horror – yet another furry little creature had formed! This one had a huge trapdoor-like mouth, a pink hue and a smug look as it loudly started saying things as if it had a Twitter feed to my innermost thoughts. It pointed at me and screamed, "He's lonely. He deletes his internet history!"

My response was a swift kick. The creature flew across the room and splatted against the wall like those goo-filled balls that stick where they splat until you pull them off or they peel off on their own. This furry little thing did just that, taking my life-size Spider-Man poster off the wall with it. The creature landed on the floor, unsplatted and unhurt, right in front of the previously hidden safe space cubbyhole. After it basically reinflated itself, it pointed and shouted, "He hides the candy in there!" as Mom picked the poster up off the floor.

But it didn't focus on any point for very long. It was

too obsessed with cataloguing all my subconscious concerns to even pause. "He's ugly. He smells weird. He only has two Instagram followers!"

I began to hyperventilate. My face was flushed and the room was spinning a bit. "Why do you change colour?" asked the asking one.

Mom pinned the poster back on the wall and grabbed up the dirty laundry still on the floor, saying, "This room is a disaster." She saw me breathing heavily and rushed over, sitting me on the bed. "It's okay, Slim. You're having a panic attack. Just breathe through it. Do you want me to get your Xanax?" I shook my head no because I knew what a panic attack was and this was not that. I would have preferred a panic attack to whatever this was.

"Just look at me, okay. Focus on me. Everything is fine," she continued. "None of this is worth getting worked up over. Just breathe."

I wanted to argue, but Mom was looking at me with her constant frenzied but exhausted concern.

I closed my eyes and breathed slowly and tried to calm my system, but when I opened my eyes, the creatures were still there and still making noises, asking questions and revealing all my worst thoughts about myself. I really wanted someone to see them too.

I wanted to shout that there were monsters in the room. But I knew she wouldn't understand. I knew I'd just get more of that look, and I knew behind it she was thinking, *Why can't you just be normal?* So instead what came out was, "There are . . . there are . . . there are . . . more candy wrappers on the nightstand." She exhaled and her shoulders slumped, and I lied some more. "I'm . . . okay. You're right. It's just a . . . panic attack." It was easier that way.

"Okay. Good. You're okay," she said as if she were trying to believe it as hard as I was trying to convince her. And with a tired sigh, she got off the bed, still holding my dirty laundry, and picked up the candy wrappers. "It's time to get ready for school."

She kissed the top of my head, which I naturally shrank away from, and left me alone with my monsters. "He's uncomfortable with physical displays of affection!" shouted the tattletale one, pointing at me.

"What's affection? Can I have some? Why are you staring at us?" asked the curious one. I didn't want to respond. I didn't want to indulge them. Hallucinating was new to me. I didn't want to make it any worse. *BEEP CRASH THUD SNIKT* added the noisy one, and I realised it was high time to get the heck out of my room.

"Should we come with you?" was the last question I heard as I hurried into the bathroom. I hopped in the shower and turned the hot water way up. Maybe somehow, I could wash away this waking nightmare. But no such luck. "What's this do?" I could hear the curious one asking from the other side of the shower curtain as it flushed the toilet. Followed by the noisy one going *FLUSH FLUSH FLUSH* as if it were a symphony of porcelain thrones.

"He pees in it!" shouted the tattletale one. Then I could see its silhouette point in my direction as it added, "And in the shower!"

I shut my eyes and took a deep breath, letting the water run hot enough to hurt a little. "It will all be okay," I told myself. "They aren't real. Just ignore them and they'll go away." I stood, head bowed, in the rushing water, trying to will these statements to be true. And when I opened my eyes again, their silhouettes were gone. I peeked out nervously from behind the shower curtain, but there were no monsters in the bathroom. I let out a huge sigh of relief. "Oh, thank God," I said as I turned the water off and grabbed a towel. "I can't handle a total psychotic break today."

"What's God?" came a voice above me. Startled, I slipped and fell out of the shower, onto the floor, pulling the curtain, curtain rod and the creatures that had crawled up onto it down on top of me. The curious one hopped over me into the tub and the other two followed. They squirted shampoo until the bottle was almost empty. It made a fart-like sound, which instantly set off the noisy one. As it blew raspberries at the top of its lungs, the curious one looked up at me and asked, "Are you God?"

But I didn't have a chance to even try to answer. The tattletale one shouted, "He doesn't know! Nobody does!" My face dropped as I realised these symptoms wouldn't be going away any time soon. The tattletale's round little ears twitched as if tuning into my thoughts like a stethoscope to a heartbeat and then it smiled and said, "Now he's wondering if there even is a God – and why it hates him."

I stood up with a heavy sigh of defeat, followed by another *SIGH*. But this one was from the noisy creature, inflating and deflating its bullfrog throat with the sound of my dismay. They all climbed out of the shower and onto the toilet to get closer to my face. The curious one wondered the exact same thing that I was wondering: "What are you going to do now?" And I surprised it and myself by knocking them all into the toilet, grabbing a plunger, and squishing them down into the bowl, as hard as I could. I slammed the lid, hit the handle and tried to flush them away for good.

I ran out of the bathroom and slammed the door shut behind me for good measure. My mother must have heard me moving because she yelled at me to hurry up. "Breakfast is getting cold!" I got back to my bedroom, got dressed and started gathering my things for school as if on autopilot. When my brain is overloaded and I feel like I'm about to fall apart, I resort to routines. I go through the motions of my normal daily activities as best I can until I start to feel myself even out again.

And that meant going to school. Because school was normal. And even though I was seeing annoying little monsters, that didn't mean I had to treat them like they were really there. I could ignore them. I had a lifetime of practice ignoring things that bother me. The chaos of bus rides and classes and students and teachers – the daily onslaught of external distractions would erase these delusions from my brain. Yeah, maybe I should have realised that my brain wasn't necessarily operating at full capacity, and maybe I should have remembered I'm not actually very good at ignoring the things that bother me, and maybe I should have tried to stay home sick or something, but I wasn't really in a rational, think-things-through headspace.

"He's trying to get rid of us!" said the tattletale as all three sopping wet monsters sloshed back into my room. I supposed I never really believed I could just flush them away. I took the textbook I'd been busy shoving into my backpack and slammed it down on the closest one, squashing it over and over again.

"GET. OUT. OF. MY. HEAD!!!" I shouted in between slams.

"You just sneezed us out of your head!" replied the tattletale as it re-formed.

"Do you want us to get back in so we can get out again?" the curious one asked.

SLAM SLAM SLAM went the noisy one. I threw the book across the room in frustration and grabbed the purple furry noisemaker by its shoulders and tried to tear it apart. But it just stretched as wide as my arms could pull it and then it snapped back into shape like a rubber band as soon as I let it go.

"Slim! Let's go. You're going to miss your bus!" Mom shouted.

Seeing no other option, I threw my backpack on and hurried for the door – but the noisy one was blocking my way. *BEEP BEEP BEEP BEEP CRASH CRASH CRASH CRASH FLUSH FLUSH FLUSH*

FLUSH SNIKT SNIKT SNIKT SIGH. It made a shampoo-fart noise when I stomped it into the floor.

"He's freaked out," told the tattletale as the noisy one re-formed with a slurping sound I hoped against hope it wouldn't start to imitate. "He's afraid we're going with him."

"Why would he be afraid of us?" asked the curious one as they all followed me out of the door. "What could go wrong?"

CHAPTER 4

THE BAD DECISION

As soon as I set foot on the bus, I knew I'd made a terrible mistake. The constant noise. The snotty faces. The weird smells. The bus was a travelling circus of potentially irritating things – and I was trapped in the centre ring. The door *SWOOSHED* shut behind me. The noisy one immediately started *SWOOSH SWOOSH SWOOSHING* in response. I watched helplessly as Mom pulled away in the other direction to go to her renovation site, our old house. What I wouldn't have given then to be able to go back to it. Things were so much simpler there. But I had no choice but to face my fate.

"Where are we going? What is this thing? Why are you cringing?" asked the curious creature as the bus driver shot me an impatient look and jerked his thumb towards an empty seat at the front. Lucy was watching me with either disgust or concern. It's hard to tell with her. But she had already taken a seat in the middle with her new soccer friends. I ducked into my seat, but with my three monsters stuffed in with me, it felt a lot more cramped than sitting alone usually does. "He has no friends," said the tattletale. "He stepped in gum. He—"

I stuck my fingers in my ears and clenched my eyes shut and I stayed like that all the way to school. When I felt the bus lurch to a stop, I ran off it so fast I actually wondered if I could lose these hallucinations if I just kept moving. But when I dared to look back, there they were, bounding right after me. There was no escape. I came to a dead stop in the middle of the foot traffic herding towards the front door of the school. No one else noticed the three annoying monsters on the sidewalk. How could no one else see these things?!

Maybe I was finally, really going insane.

"Why aren't you moving?" asked the curious one.

"He doesn't like us," responded the tattletale.

The curious one seemed shocked and hurt by this. It looked up at me with its big, wide eyes and asked, "Why don't you like us?" It sounded so sincere I almost felt bad for it, like it was real. But, as if answering on my behalf, the noisy one went back to *BEEP BEEP BEEPING* as if it couldn't not make noise and that was its natural default. I slumped my shoulders and dragged myself into school with everyone else.

Even under the most normal circumstances, school was a challenge. But normally when I had serious anxiety or a full-blown panic attack, the things that triggered it were just temporary – like the booger that Otis flicked on me. Eventually, I could get away. But that wasn't the case with these furry figments of my imagination.

The noisy one mimicked every locker slam and bag zipping I heard, loudly and proudly.

The curious one bounced around in front of me asking questions without seeming to breathe. "What's homework? Can I eat that? Why are they staring at you?" The kids in the hall were giving me strange looks as I unsuccessfully tried to swat and kick away the monsters no one else could see.

The tattletale had somehow tapped a whole vein of new secrets and it couldn't spill them fast enough. "He wet the bed till he was seven. He's wearing yesterday's underwear. He hoards Twizzlers."

Mortified to hear all my shortcomings catalogued at full volume, even though no one else could hear any of this, I swung my backpack off my shoulder, unzipped it, dumped my books out and snatched up the tattletale in one swift motion. Then I zipped it shut, which muffled the blabbermouth enough to make its monologue of my secrets almost bearable. Unfortunately, I did this right on the perfectly trendy shoes of Heather Hu and her clonelike horde, who looked at me like . . . well, like I was nuts. "Here we have a garden variety dork in its native environment," said Heather as she recorded my behaviour on her phone like it was some sort of demented nature documentary. The trendoids who followed her were delighted. I was just annoyed.

And then it happened again. I didn't mean to, but I couldn't stop it. I sneezed on her. And I have to admit it felt kind of good. She squealed and cursed and stomped away only to be replaced a moment later by a red-furred, blue-horned creature with an "over it" expression plastered on its face. The snarky-looking monster gave me a long side-eye glance and then rolled its eyes away and said, "Not even worth it."

BRRRRING! The bell rang, warning me that I had to get to class. Heather's horde stepped over my books, which I gathered frantically in my other hand as the curious creature wondered, "What's a dork? Am I a dork? Is dork a bad thing?"

As I stumbled down the hall, I could hear the tattletale trying to comment on the situation, but thankfully its monologue was muffled inside my backpack. *BRRRRING!* I was already late! I started running past all the other kids who were still walking calmly to class and I tripped over someone's bag on the floor, face-planting and skidding across the cold tiles to the utter joy of everyone who saw it. I rolled over to find the noisy one climbing onto my chest. It opened its trapdoor mouth and . . . *BRRRRING!* I smacked it away, splatting it against a locker. But by the time I got up and gathered my scattered books and dignity, the noisemaker had already peeled free from the lockers and re-formed like an inflating balloon. *BRRRRING!* But this time it actually was the bell and I actually was late.

I hurried into homeroom while Mrs Bowers's back was turned and made it to my seat without getting caught for being tardy. I reached into my backpack to get a pen and inadvertently released the tattletale. It scrambled out and joined the other creatures all around my desk. As Mrs Bowers started roll call, I took a deep, cleansing breath, and tried to calm down and focus. I was almost getting used to the chorus of random noises and annoying questions and personal revelations from the monsters when a spine-tingling *SNIFFLE* cut through the ruckus. I looked at the noisy one accusingly, but its ears were aimed behind me, excited to hear a new noise to mimic.

I turned to glare at Otis Miller, and was surprised

to see that this time he looked genuinely sick. He even had a mini-pack of tissues on his desk. Otis looked at me sheepishly. "My mom said without a fever I'm not contagious and can't stay at home."

Before I could respond, Mrs Bowers yelled, "MR PICKINGS!" I spun round to face the front and shouted "HERE!" while instantly fearing the use of my last name would inspire someone in this room to start in with the nose-picking taunts again. But Otis was too down with his cold to bother. Instead, he let out another shiver-inducing *SNIFFLE SNIFFLE SNEEZE* from behind me. I could feel little droplets of stray spittle hit my neck and reflexively spun round again to say something, but I just responded with a massive sneeze of my own.

"I knew I was contagious!" blurted Otis as he raised his hand. "Can I go to the nurse?"

Mrs Bowers dismissed him and Otis fled the room without even offering me a tissue. Normally I would have freaked out, but today I had way bigger worries. I just wiped my neck with my sleeve as the curious creature wondered, "If he's contagious, what am I?"

"You're annoying," said the tattletale. "We all are."

"That's an understatement," commented the snarky one.

The curious one looked almost as if its feelings were hurt again.

I tried to focus on the announcements Mrs Bowers was reading out loud, but then I heard the *SNIFF SNIFF SNIFF* start again. I looked accusingly at the noisy one, but it was busy *BEEP BEEP BEEPING*. I cringed as I realised what had just happened. I turned round towards Otis's empty desk, terrified of what I knew I'd see — another translucent glob of goo. This one had sprouted fur and arms and was stretching its body upward. It had a big, pink nose to go with its droopy, watery eyes and floppy ears. It sniffled and sneezed and wiped its nose in its own fur. For a moment it looked content, but then it sneezed and started the whole process over again. It was one sticky-looking, snot-hardened, green-furred, monster hallucination.

"Why does that happen?" asked the curious one, observing its new colleague.

"Because he's easily annoyed," chimed in the tattletale. "He's also pissing off the teacher," it added as Mrs Bowers gave me another stern look.

I slunk down in my seat, trying to ignore the sniffling one too. But that was hard to do. The noisy one had latched onto its sniffle sounds and they were sitting on either side of my chair back. It was *SNIFF*

SNIFF SNIFF in one ear and *SNIFF SNIFF SNIFF* in the other. Like an echo chamber of grossness that prevented me from actually paying attention to whatever Mrs Bowers was going on about.

Science class afforded me a bit of a break since everyone was focused on a test and that meant they were unlikely to create any new annoyances. The room was quiet, at least to everyone else. Me, I was swarmed by monsters. And the relative silence amplified the sloshing, chomping, gulping sounds Mr Schwartz made while eating a messy tuna sandwich at his desk. Every swallow seemed to last for ever down his ostrich-like throat. And the noisy one's exuberant mimicry of the sound caused me to shudder and gag.

"As if you sound any better when you eat," noted the snarky one with a dismissive face. "Also, you're totally failing your test," it said without even bothering to look at the test I was too distracted to work on.

The curious one made its way over to the Evolution of Man poster. It looked at me, then the poster, then at me again, suddenly understanding something and wondering, "If that's what *you* came from, then what did *I* come from?"

"Boogers!" shouted the tattletale. And, as if on cue, the sniffling one perked up and sneezed right in my face. I wiped it off, totally grossed out. But as I did, my annoyance suddenly morphed into remembrance.

"I got sprayed. With PVZ! They said it . . . absorbs irritation," I said to myself, causing Mr Schwartz to *SHUSH* me from the front of the room, which got the noisy creature *SHUSH SHUSH SHUSHING* me too.

"Is that how we got here?" asked the curious one.

"He's figuring it out right now," said the tattletale.

And it was right. I ducked down closer to my desk, mind spinning, replaying the events in my mind, piecing together what little information I had. Everything that annoys me makes me sneeze. Then I hallucinate a creature that does that annoying thing. And this didn't happen to me until I got sprayed. "It had to be the PVZ," I reasoned to myself. Then I said PVZ again, but this time, I sounded it out. "The . . . peeves." I sat up in my desk with a grand realisation. "They're peeves! Real-life peeves!"

The creatures all nodded like this was news to them, but made total sense. They were furry little living embodiments of my personal peeves. Noisy Peeve – the purple one with the satellite ears and throat like a bullfrog; Asking Peeve – the blue one with massive eyes and perpetually perplexed expression; Telling Peeve – the pink fluffy one with a Muppet-like blabbermouth that spewed my actual thoughts and feelings; Snarky Peeve – the blue-horned red devil-looking thing with the bad attitude; and Sniffle Peeve – the sticky, crusty green one with the perpetually runny nose.

"I'm sneezing peeves," I said out loud. "I'm—"

"Disturbing the class," interjected Mr Schwartz, who was now looming over me as if he'd been trying to get my attention for far too long. The whole class was staring at me, snickering. And that's when I realised I had been audibly mumbling like a madman. Mr Schwartz ended that with a definitive, "Stop it!"

As I made my way to social studies, I was still trying to wrap my head round the big revelation. I was seeing actual peeves. I had to call Dad. I had to let him know what the PVZ did to me! I stopped outside the classroom and pulled out my phone, which I knew was not allowed while classes were in session – but kids did it all the time. No one ever got in trouble. Seriously, no one – until, of course, I did. Principal Waters came round the corner and snatched it out of my hand as if this were his brand-new mission in life. "No phones, Steven. Or was it Steve?" he asked.

"Slim," I corrected him. "And this is an emergency! I had an experimental anti-anxiety treatment blow up in my face and now I'm seeing . . ." I stopped myself because a well-worn "heard-it-all-and-doesn't-buy-it" expression quickly crossed Principal Waters's face. He never would have believed me if I had told him the truth. "I need to call my dad," I said. "I'm . . . sick," I added, with an unconvincing cough.

"Looks like a case of 'new-kid-itis' to me," said Principal Waters as he turned me round and opened the door to social studies for me. "The only cure for that is to go back to class," he concluded. "You can have your phone back after school."

I watched him disappear down the hall and realised I'd just have to make it through the rest of the day on my own. Dad would take me back to Clarity Labs after school. They'd have a cure there. They had to, I figured. Because if they didn't, I was pretty sure I'd really go crazy.

In the meantime, I'd been assigned to work with genetically gifted Chance Chandler on a project exploring the chapter on "Individual Development and Identity".

"Do I develop? Do I have identity?" asked Asking Peeve as Ms Mayfarb walked around the room in her oversize cardigan and waist-length dreadlocks, spouting off her own questions to "help inspire" our projects.

"How do individuals grow and change? Why do they behave the way they do? What factors in society and politics and culture influence how people develop over time?" she asked as she pushed Chance's feet off his desk and removed his baseball cap.

"Sorry, Ms Mayfarb. I just like having my thinking cap on," he said with a flawless smile. And I swear half the class swooned. Even Ms Mayfarb softened and put the hat back on his head. Right before she looked at me and said, "Take notes from this one, Slim. He's a charmer."

And once she had moved on, Chance pushed his work my way and said, "She's right. You should take the notes." Then he reclined in his seat with another self-confident grin I couldn't relate to and added, "I can tell from your expression that you're more of the thinker type anyway."

"More like an overthinker type," snorted Snarky Peeve from below our pushed-together desks. And neither one of them were wrong. I was thinking so hard I had actually broken a sweat. How could I be expected to work with Noisy, Asking, Telling, Snarky and Sniffle Peeves on my case? And with no help from Chance, who was apparently so well liked he could get away with doing anything – and by anything, I mean he could get away with doing nothing. He might be popular, but he's also lazy.

"Thanks, bro," added Chance as he tipped his baseball cap over his eyes to nap. Good thing he did, or he would have got a sneeze in the face.

As I left social studies, I had roly-poly Lazy Peeve literally hanging off me. Three times the size of the other peeves with tiny ears and sleepy eyes, Lazy was like a gravelly-grey-coloured blob of extra-heavy deadweight. It couldn't even be bothered to keep its own tongue in its mouth. It just lolled out of the corner from exhaustion as it forced me to drag it around. I'm not even sure how I made it to the gym with it clinging to my leg. I was just relieved to discover that we had a chilled-out student teacher sub for phys ed, who excitedly announced, "Wallyball!"

With six peeves swarming me, bugging me and hanging off me, I was getting desperate and Wallyball gave me an idea. Just in case you've never played, Wallyball is kind of like volleyball, except you play with a big beach ball that you can hit off the walls before you hit it over the net. It's totally disorganised and totally out of control. At least, that's how it was with this student teacher sub in charge. Everyone was already freaking out in the middle of the court, chasing after and swatting the ball.

It was exactly the opening I needed.

Once I was changed and got out of the locker room, I joined the other kids in the spare room next to the gym. I don't even know what that space was supposed to be, but with its high ceilings and mats everywhere, it felt custom-made for Wallyball. I was finally able to shake Lazy Peeve off my leg as I ducked under the net strung across the middle of the room. The peeve lay down right on the floor, as if it'd already had the hardest day ever. And I was so frustrated that I kicked it as hard as I could. I wanted to send it splatting against the gym wall, but it was so much heavier than the other peeves that it just sort of flopped over onto its face.

"Why'd you do that?" asked Asking Peeve, but I was inspired. I ran around the court like a madman grabbing, throwing and kicking my peeves in any direction I could. I punted one over the net and watched it *THWACK* against a wall, I tossed another through the portable basketball hoop in the corner for a perfect *SWOOSH* and *SPLAT* on the floor, and then I kicked one right into a pile of mats that I was sure would bury it for ever. But no matter how hard I tried, my peeves would just peel free and reinflate themselves. Then they'd go right back to annoying me. By the end of the Wallyball game, they were all standing and I was exhausted.

We returned to the locker room as the period wound down. The rest of the guys dressed quickly and headed off to their next class. But I couldn't peel myself off the bench. My mind was spinning. My inner monologue was going bonkers. And I was feeling desperate and defeated.

"This is crazy," I said, which prompted Asking Peeve to wonder, "What is crazy?"

And Telling Peeve answered, "He thinks *he* is," pointing right in my face.

"It's not a good look on you," cracked Snarky Peeve.

And that's when I lost it. "*I'M* not crazy!" I screamed. "*THIS* is crazy!" I shouted, standing up, motioning around me at all of them. But as soon as the words were out of my mouth, I wondered if it were true. I mean, what else would you call a boy who is being hounded by monsters only he can see?

"Or maybe I am crazy." I sighed. "Do crazy people know that they're crazy? Maybe the fact that I think I'm not crazy means I actually am crazy. . . ." I trailed off.

"What's this for?" asked Asking Peeve, pulling a jockstrap from a locker as the other peeves bounced around. Asking Peeve pulled the jockstrap over its head for a moment, and I couldn't help but burst out laughing. There was nothing left to do.

"What's so funny?" asked Asking Peeve, but I just looked at it, peeking out from that jockstrap, and started laughing even harder.

"I'm talking to my invisible peeves!" I yelled in hysterics as I changed out of my gym clothes. But then that really hit me. I stopped laughing and sat down again. "Ugh. I'm *talking to my invisible peeves.* I'm so crazy I'm actually annoying myself," I said, wiping tears from my eyes. And then I sneezed yet another peeve – one that literally bounced off the walls even before it fully formed. It was bright yellow with jagged fur. It looked a bit like it had been electrocuted. It had massive spinning eyes, though one was smaller than the other, and a creepy, deranged smile that nearly wrapped round its whole face. It was screaming hysterically, but whatever it was trying to say made no sense at all. And it barely stayed still long enough for me to hear clearly anyway. "Grun grun bagga boo!" was all I could make out.

Crazy Peeve – wonderful.

I stumbled out into the hall, still trying to get my arm through my shirtsleeve while carrying my backpack and gym clothes in the other hand. Lunch had started while I was still in the locker room, and I was in no hurry to get to a cafeteria filled with infinite possibilities of further annoyance. Crazy Peeve already seemed to be everywhere at once, making faces, speaking gibberish at full volume and continuing to bounce off the walls. I tried to convince myself that having a Crazy Peeve didn't mean I was actually crazy when I suddenly became aware that everyone was staring at me. Whispering. Pointing. Snapping photos. I really didn't think having my arm stuck in my shirt was that big a deal. I finally got it through and grabbed my gym clothes out of my other hand to stuff in my backpack. That's when I realised I wasn't just holding my gym clothes. I was also holding my TROUSERS.

I looked down in complete horror to discover I was rocking an utterly humiliating boxers and sneakers look for the entire school to see. "That's also not a good look on you," said Snarky Peeve.

Everyone was pointing and laughing. "Trouserless Pickings!" shouted Otis Miller from the door of the nurse's office before laughing so hard he hacked up a goober. I could feel my chest constrict, my heart race, the jitters rise . . . the PANIC. I had to run. I had to hide! I ducked through a nearby door and found myself in a storage closet. I could hear everyone laughing even harder as they realised I was hiding, but I didn't care. I needed a minute to breathe. To stop shaking. To put my trousers on.

Alone with a bunch of cleaning supplies and seven annoying peeves, the questions and worries started to flood out.

"Why are we in here?"

"He's embarrassed."

"More like sweaty and weird."

"Grun grun go closet boink!" Crazy Peeve ricocheted around, knocking mops and buckets everywhere.

The sawdust stuff that janitors use whenever someone throws up in school showered down over me. Which was fitting because I totally felt like human vomit. In my first two days I went from "Booger Boy" to "Trouserless Pickings." My life was over.

I sat down and shut my eyes. I clamped my hands over my ears and tried to block out the world. Breathe. Breathe. Breathe. I was trying so hard to calm down that I was freaking myself out even worse. But then, for a brief moment, it seemed like everything had stopped. I let go of my ears and actually heard nothing.

I opened my eyes, hoping they'd gone away, but instead, the peeves had just stopped their *peeving* and were staring at me.

"Why are you doing that?" asked Asking Peeve, almost like it cared. And for the first time since this started, I answered it directly. "Because you're driving me crazy. Literally. Talking to my peeves officially makes me crazy!" I shouted, causing the puke-absorbent sawdust to flutter off my head like dandruff. And then, as if to emphasise the point, the rest of the peeves went right back to doing what they do.

And that's when it hit me. A roll of paper towels. Right in the head. I looked up at Crazy Peeve doing a crazy dance and realised that it was responsible for knocking the towels over on me. I was about to grab the roll and chuck it back at the peeve as hard as I could when I really realised that Crazy Peeve had knocked it over. He'd knocked it over? "How can you actually knock things over if you're only a crazy hallucination?" I asked.

"What's a hallucination?" asked Asking Peeve.

"Not us," said Telling Peeve, confirming what I had just realised.

"Holy crap," I said as confusion, relief and horror rushed over me all at once. "You're all . . . REAL?!"

I backed into the shelf, causing another half-dozen rolls to fall on me. But I didn't care. "I'm not crazy," I said to myself. If they're real enough to knock over paper towel rolls, then it's not crazy to talk to them. Asking Peeve examined the puke dust, pondering this new information like the beginnings of an existential crisis of its own. "If we are real and you are not crazy, then why are you so upset?" it asked.

I didn't answer because I was too busy processing the fact that if I wasn't insane, then these invisible monsters were really there. And it occurred to me that this didn't necessarily make my situation any better. In fact, it probably made it worse. Much, much worse.

"This is the absolute worst day of my life," I concluded.

"Whatever," said Snarky Peeve. "It could always get worse."

"How could things get worse?" wondered Asking Peeve, and as if on cue, there was a knock on the door. The peeves all turned to look at it.

"Slim? It's Suzie. Are you okay?"

"There you go," I said, realising that I was trouserless, panicked and peeve-infected. "That's how it gets worse."

CHAPTER 5

THE CLOSET CASE

Before I could answer or hide, the knob turned and Suzie stepped into the closet. The room filled with her signature scent, which was strangely comforting. I stood up and tried to find my balance and to seem okay. But the weird thing was that Suzie seemed okay with me not seeming okay. She could have said a million things to make this worse, but instead she said, "Bad day, huh?"

If she could have seen the peeves all around us, she wouldn't have had to ask. But the fact that she did ask, when everyone else either made fun of me or ignored me altogether, made me feel warm inside. "Yeah, it's been . . . crazy." That's what I said. Like a real conversation. All of a sudden I could breathe again. I felt like maybe I would be okay. That's when I noticed something odd: the peeves had stopped being annoying. They were all sitting calmly around Suzie's feet.

"Do you want to talk about it?" Suzie looked at me like she was really trying to figure me out.

"Why would you want to talk about *me*?" I asked and instantly regretted it.

Suzie got a little shy and said, "I dunno, you're different. I like that. And you seem upset." I'm pretty sure I smiled, but it didn't last because I suddenly became aware that I was alone in the closet with Suzie and I had no trousers on. I scrambled to get dressed, nearly falling into a shelf while doing so. Suzie averted her eyes, kind of giggling, but not in a mean way. She seemed a little embarrassed too. "The older kids use this place for kissing and stuff," she explained. I could feel the blood rush to my face. Of course the first time I was alone with a girl in a kissing closet was when she was checking to see if I'd lost my mind.

Trousers on, I tried to feign a little dignity, but Suzie looked down and right back up at me real quick. "Do you feel a draught in here?" she said with a smile. My fly was down. When I zipped it, I expected to hear that *ZIP* sound repeated by Noisy Peeve, but all of the peeves were suddenly acting like someone had shot them with tranquilisers. And every move Suzie made, they just sort of shuffled along behind her.

"You don't see anything . . . strange . . . in here, do you?" I asked, hoping for once to not be totally alone in my waking nightmare. Suzie looked around, right past all of the peeves, then up at the shelves with a shrug.

"I haven't been in here in a while. I like what they've done with the place," said Suzie, totally unfazed by any of this.

"You . . . you come here a lot?" I squeaked nervously.

She shot me a look. "Not for *that!*" she said. But then she cocked her head thoughtfully. "Not that I wouldn't under the right circumstances," she added with a wink. Or maybe she just blinked. I don't know. Either way, I gulped in response. She walked towards me. Getting closer than we'd ever been. I got so nervous I swear I could taste my own tongue. But then she reached for the supply shelf behind me and pulled out a stack of comics and a little flashlight and I felt stupid-stupid-stupid for ever thinking anything like that was even possible.

"I sometimes hide in here during lunch when I need a break from . . . well, from being me," she said, looking down in a vulnerable way I didn't expect from her. She seemed so perfect and popular and put together. Why would she possibly need a break from any of that? "I found it during the pudding trousers incident I told you about," she answered as if reading my mind. "It was school picture day and I looked like I crapped myself and everyone was chanting, 'Suzie Skidmark'. This was the only logical place to go. And now it's kind of . . . I dunno . . . my safe space."

I could not believe that she had a safe space too. I wanted to tell her everything. "You like comics?" was the dumb thing I asked instead.

"Um, yeah. Mostly indie stuff. I like them dark and funny," she answered, handing me a comic about a creepy little dead girl. "My dads think I'm too young for that one, but I'm kind of obsessed." I flipped through the pages, not registering any of it because my mind was spinning about everything that was happening. My peeves were still chilling out at Suzie's feet. I was totally confused by their change of behaviour, but I wasn't about to question it. I was thankful for the break and didn't want to scare away the one person who kind of seemed to get me.

"So . . . what's going on with you?" Suzie asked.

"I . . . don't really know," I replied.

She nodded. "Yeah, I get that." The moment lingered a bit and I think we both became hyper-aware of our proximity in the kissing closet. The bell rang and snapped me out of my dopey stupor. "That's my cue," said Suzie as she slipped out the door. "Maybe get your shirt right side out and put your other shoe on and then we can walk to class together?" The door closed behind her, right on the peeves that had tried to follow. I stood there in shock.

"She smells good," said Telling Peeve, suddenly awake again.

ZIP ZIP ZIPPPPPPP. Noisy Peeve woke up with a delayed reaction to my trousers incident.

"Why does she make you act that way?" asked Asking Peeve over Sniffle Peeve's sniffs and sneezes. I wasn't sure how I was acting, but I did have butterflies in my stomach and a pleasant warmth in my cheeks. I fixed my clothes as quickly as possible, but Crazy Peeve was bouncing off the walls again and Lazy Peeve kept pulling on my shirt-tail, slowing me down.

"He has a crush on her," announced Telling Peeve. And it was right. I did have a crush on her — big-time.

"Good luck with that," Snarky Peeve muttered. And I knew it was probably right as well, but I also realised that Suzie was pretty much the only person today who didn't cause me to create a new peeve. So when I got out of the closet and found her waiting for me, I felt very lucky that she wanted to walk me to class.

Being near Suzie, I was able to get through algebra without humiliating myself again. That gave me hope. Maybe I could control them. But Suzie and I parted ways before the final class of the day. "Hope you feel better," she said, waving goodbye as she walked away down the hall. My peeves wandered after her until she turned the corner, out of sight. Then they snapped out of it and came running back at me, acting up all over again.

Mrs Bowers barely acknowledged me as I returned to her room for English class and sat down, removing the "Trousers-Free Zone" sign someone had placed on the desk. Sometimes one of the benefits of being "problematic" is that teachers only have a certain amount of bandwidth to deal with you before they need a mental break, and I think I used up my weekly allotment from Mrs Bowers with my panic attack the day before. While she started her lesson, kids were passing phones back and forth sharing photos of my newest humiliation and snickering, which seemed extra unfair considering my phone had just been confiscated. Mrs Bowers didn't even seem to notice. Or maybe she didn't care. Maybe I used up her bandwidth for the entire class too. As Noisy Peeve mimicked the buzzes and chimes of texts being exchanged, I knew I was destined to be another meme by the end of the day. So I just zoned out, letting my peeves run wild around me, eagerly awaiting the bell that would get me one step closer to freedom.

When it finally rang, I ran for history class. On the chalkboard, the teacher had written: "Quote of the day: Those who do not learn history are doomed to repeat it." This seemed particularly relevant as my peeves continued to swarm me. Despite my best efforts to learn how and why this was happening, I just kept repeating the same mistakes. Now there were seven of them running amok as our teacher, Mrs Patel, strode down the aisles, collecting our homework. I searched my backpack for my assignment, which I had actually done last night, but couldn't seem to find now.

Mrs Patel was almost as small as some of the students, but she moved and spoke twice as fast as any of us. She looked like she was two moves away from winning a game and couldn't wait to finish you off. And right now, with my papers splayed everywhere and my backpack gaping open, I was slowing her down. "Steven, the assignment. Now," she said. I tried to block out the peeves and dig through my bag as quickly as I could, which only made Mrs Patel grow impatient. "In ten seconds you'll get a zero," she added, tapping her foot as if she were counting down. That just made me frantic.

"Why is she doing that?"

"To scare him."

"Nothing is scarier than those ugly orange shoes."

"Grun grun bonker bong."

BEEP BEEP ZIP SWOOSH CRASH FLUSH SIGH.

My peeves were suddenly in full chorus mode.

"Do you have it or not?" nagged Mrs Patel. And I sneezed right on her shoes.

The translucent goo slid off the hideous orange footwear, sprouting fur of the same colour, and then eyes and ears and arms and two little blue horns just like Snarky Peeve. Its mouth was set in a permanent frown and it picked right up where Mrs Patel left off. "Did you do it, did you do it, did you do it, did you do it?" I smacked it with a binder, sending it across the room to splat against the chalkboard. Everyone was too distracted by my sudden jerky movement to notice that Nagging Peeve's peeling, sliding body just smeared most of the quote off the board, leaving only a few legible fragments that read, "u . . . are . . . doomed". Nagging Peeve reinflated behind Mrs Patel's desk and came back for more.

Mrs Patel wiped my booger juice off her shoes with a handkerchief and then noticed a paper stuck to the back of my binder. "Is that it?" she asked. I flipped it round to find the assignment held to the cover by something gooey. It didn't take a genius to figure out that Sniffle Peeve had got its nose all over it. "I don't have all day," nagged Mrs Patel again, so I had no choice but to peel it loose and hand it over. Mrs Patel grabbed the paper impatiently, but then recoiled at how soggy and sticky it was. "This is . . . wet! I don't accept wet homework, Mr Pickings!" she shouted as she slammed it down on my desk. "You've wasted my time and your classmates' time and your own time because now you get to do it again, for no credit," she said, already moving up the aisle to collect the rest of the students' work.

I stared at the ruined homework like it was a scientific breakthrough. "Why doesn't she like wet homework?" asked Asking Peeve from atop my desk, where it had watched the whole thing. It was hard enough to accept that these peeves were actually real, but Mrs Patel clearly touched Sniffle Peeve's snot. Which meant even though I was still the only one who could see or hear them, I wasn't the only one who could be affected by them. A crusty green paw reached up from below the desk and gently pulled the assignment away from me. A moment later I heard Sniffle Peeve blowing its nose in it.

The final bell rang and I ran out of class. Normally

I'd stop at my locker, but it was blocked by a gaggle of kids, and I didn't even want to know what kind of peeve would pop up from my personal space issues if I tried to push through. So I hurried to the principal's office, retrieved my phone, and ran outside to call for help.

But all I got was Dad's voicemail. I hung up and called Mom next. Same thing. "Why aren't they answering? What are they doing instead? Shouldn't they be helping you?" asked Asking Peeve with seemingly genuine concern.

"I'm not even sure if they could," I responded without thinking.

"Why not?"

"They can't see you. And most people don't acknowledge what they can't see," I said as I started to text Dad instead, "let alone know what to do about it."

"How do you know that?"

"Because I live it every day," I answered, surprising myself. I stopped mid-text and looked up at Asking Peeve, realising something I was feeling but had never quite put into words before. "No one can see what I deal with, so no one gets what's going on with me," I said, astounded by the simple revelation.

"He's having a breakthrough instead of a breakdown!" shouted Telling Peeve.

Asking Peeve sighed, like it could relate. And I couldn't believe it, but the sympathy actually sort of helped a little.

That's when I noticed Lucy, already waiting for our bus that hadn't pulled up yet. But something wasn't right. Even from far away, I could see that something was bothering her. And not the kind of something that other people can see. She was standing next to her annoying new friend Maya. "I can't wait to order those new cleats. And those hair ties. And sweatbands. We'll be total twinsies!" exclaimed Maya as she ran past me to talk to the rest of their team. But the strange thing was that Lucy didn't go with her. She stayed by the kerb, alone, which was totally unlike her.

"You should hurry. You're gonna be late. You're gonna miss the bus," whined Nagging Peeve. But I wasn't really paying attention to it because I'd noticed that Lucy wasn't completely alone after all. Right where Maya had been standing, there was a teal-coloured, two-headed peeve that Lucy kept turning her back on.

"Where did *that* peeve come from?" asked Asking Peeve.

I didn't remember sneezing out a two-headed one. Lucy stealthily swatted at its heads, trying to shoo it away. The peeve just mimicked her move by swatting right back at her. Lucy dodged it and stepped back, looking around to make sure no one saw her freak out, and then crossed her arms as if she were going to be able to just will it away. But the two-headed peeve stepped back, crossed its arms, and made the same worried expression she wore – but on both of its faces. Lucy looked around again to make sure no one could see before laying some pretty bad words on it. But the peeve seemed unfazed. It just said the same exact words right back at her, one head at a time.

Across the sidewalk, our eyes met. And Lucy's jaw dropped. It seemed like she could see all the peeves swarming me. Then she looked back up at my equally shocked face, and I realised, yes, she actually could. "You can see them too?!" I shouted.

"Oh my God, they're all over you!" Lucy cried. "I was in study hall and Maya kept agreeing with me and repeating my stories to everyone else after I already told them and asking where I got my new cleats and then I sneezed and . . ."

"You developed a Copy Peeve," I finished, staring at the double-headed monster that was currently repeating everything Lucy had just said for the second time with its second head.

Lucy looked at all of my peeves, and for a moment, she was even more panicked than me. "I just have this one. And it's the worst! But you have so many! WHAT'S WRONG WITH US?!"

The "us" part made me want to cry. For the first time all day, I felt like I wasn't alone. "We have peeves," I said.

"Peeves?" she echoed in confusion, trying to put it all together.

"Peeves? Peeves?" repeated Copy Peeve.

"Grun grun boinker noggin!" added Crazy Peeve, as if to reiterate how annoying they could all be.

"I think it was the PVZ. At Clarity Labs," I explained. "It did something to me. To us! We have to get back there, but Mom and Dad aren't answering their phones!"

"Remember the lab rats were going crazy?" she said. "They must have been dealing with their own . . . peeves." And Copy Peeve repeated everything she said and every gesture she made. Including the moment Lucy looked me dead in the eye and said, "You don't think this is permanent, do you?"

I could feel the colour drain from my face. "I . . . hadn't thought of that." I must have looked really afraid because Lucy gave me the super-annoyed look she saves for when I'm too freaked out to function.

"I'm too overwhelmed to deal with you being afraid of everythi—" she started before letting out a huge SNEEZE. And we both stared silently as that sneeze sprouted white fur and formed into the tiny, constantly shivering, nervously bug-eyed Fraidy Peeve. It instantly ran for cover behind Lucy's leg. Then it looked up at her, as if *she* were the monster, and SHRIEKED in terror. Lucy squealed in response and punted Fraidy Peeve up into the flagpole at the centre of the courtyard. It was a good kick. Lucy really is a great soccer player.

"How did she get peeves?" The question came from Asking Peeve. And it was a good one. If I was the only one who inhaled the PVZ, then how was it spreading?

"Maybe the PVZ got into me too? I was in the hallway right afterwards. And the stuff is airborne," Lucy reasoned through her panic.

"So is that how *they* got peeves too?" Asking Peeve then wondered, pointing back towards the school. We turned round to see two giant peeves harassing Otis, whose trip to the nurse's office clearly didn't make anything better for him. Chance was being chased by a peeve that seemed to be flirting with him unrelentingly. And Heather came running out with her own peeve trailing behind her, trying to keep up. One of her un-peeved horde was taking video of her for a change, which made Heather snap at her friend in frustration and sneeze right in her face, seemingly answering Asking Peeve's question.

"It's the sneezes!" I realised. All the kids I sneezed around earlier now had peeves of their own, and now they were sneezing and spreading them too. The entire crowd of kids waiting for and climbing onto buses seemed to be coming down with a case of peeves. "The sneezes must be releasing the PVZ back into the air!"

A SCREAM came from up above. A panicked, peeve-ridden kid had crashed into the flagpole, causing Fraidy Peeve to plummet to the ground, wrapped in the flag. Fraidy popped out of the crumpled flag and ran around screaming. It bounced like a fear-induced pinball off other kids and other peeves until it came back to us and clung to Lucy's leg for protection.

And that's when it hit us:

"PEEVES ARE CONTAGIOUS!" we both shouted.

"PEEVES ARE CONTAGIOUS! PEEVES ARE CONTAGIOUS!" echoed Copy Peeve, which prompted Telling Peeve to look around at the chaos and say exactly what I was thinking: "And we're spreading fast."

CHAPTER 6

THE INFESTATION

As we stood outside the school, still trying to comprehend the fact that we'd infected other kids with peeves, we also saw that their behaviour hadn't gone unnoticed. Uninfected people were baffled by the screaming, crying kids running scattershot all over the place. Otis had found a safe corner, where he curled into a ball and yelled at the school nurse to call 911. Nearby, Chance was being smothered by Flirting Peeve and Heather was coming undone while her horde just filmed her reaction, smiling like they knew they'd found social media gold.

"Why can't *everyone* see this?" asked Lucy. Principal Waters was running around, trying to calm people down, but every time he'd get one of the peeved kids separated from the others, another kid would sneeze and freak out at a peeve of their own.

"Who are you talking to?!" shouted Mrs Bowers. "There's nothing here. Everyone needs to calm down!"

she demanded as the school nurse stepped away from Otis and actually did pull out her phone to call 911.

"There's an outbreak of . . . something bad . . . at New Old Wayford Middle School," I could hear her say. "I don't know what it is . . . Everyone is just losing their minds! You need to send help as soon as possible!" she shouted as she ran past us to tend to another kid who fell over while fleeing his peeves.

"Only people who have peeves can see peeves!" I shouted.

"We need to get out of here!" said Lucy, a thought instantly echoed by both of Copy Peeve's heads. She kicked Copy Peeve into the road, where it splatted against a bus that had just pulled up. I was frozen in shock at the sight of so many other people who had no idea what the heck was wrong with them. It was total chaos. "It's like *Lord of the Flies* come to life," I said in a daze. Lucy grabbed my arm and we navigated the crowd as best we could with Lazy Peeve clinging to my backpack and Fraidy Peeve clamped to Lucy's leg. Copy Peeve was still stuck to the front grille of the school bus. We blew past the bus driver and rushed inside, but he stepped off to see what all the excitement was about.

A few kids had already boarded the bus and they

were totally freaked by the scene outside. They had no peeves, so I could tell they hadn't been infected yet. "It's the end times," whispered a terrified boy I didn't know.

Another girl corrected him. "Don't be silly. This is clearly an *Invasion of the Body Snatchers* situation." Maya had taken a seat in the middle and waved Lucy over, but Lucy was not about to risk sneezing out another Copy Peeve. So she shoved me into a seat at the front and squeezed in next to me. It was a tight fit, but I didn't care because at least I wasn't alone for a change. Sniffle Peeve wiped its nose on Lucy's sleeve, as if welcoming her to my nightmare.

"We should go. We should go. We should go," said Nagging Peeve as Mrs Patel tried to stop two kids from getting into a fight in front of the buses. I could see she was being hounded by her own peeve. It was screaming, "I forgot my homework. The dog ate it. My mom wrote a note." It looked an awful lot like me. I was so distracted I barely heard the *SNEEZE*.

"Oh my God, WHAT IS THAT?!" screamed Maya from behind us. She launched out of her seat, wiping her nose and looking back at a moving glob of translucent goo that morphed into a peeve of her own. She backed down the aisle towards us, but she could suddenly see our peeves too. She screamed again and ran off the bus with her peeve in pursuit. The driver bounded back on board, pulling the door shut with a *SWOOSH* that Noisy Peeve couldn't resist.

"I don't know what's happening, but we're out of here!" the driver said as he put the bus in gear and took off. "I don't get paid enough for this."

The school faded into the background, and the driver looked in his rear-view mirror at us. "Four kids, two stops, and then a six-pack to forget this," he said as Lucy and I looked over our seat at the scared boy and know-it-all girl who stared right back as if we were dangerous. Lucy slumped down in our seat. She wasn't used to that sort of attention. "They can't even see my peeves and they still gave me the stink eye."

"Welcome to my life," I replied. We sat for a quiet beat, letting it all sink in. But only we were quiet. Our peeves were busy doing their peeve-thing.

"Why are they afraid of us?" asked Asking Peeve as it peeked over the seat at the other kids.

"Because we're different," responded Telling Peeve before pointing right in my face again and saying, "His thumbnails are too big. He dances to Taylor Swift in his room. His sister hates him." That last one got Lucy's attention, but before she could say anything,

92

Crazy Peeve popped up between us, staring right in her face, spinning its googly eyes and rambling absolute gibberish while smushing her cheeks together.

She shoved it away, but it came right back. "They seem to thrive on being annoying," she said, pulling Fraidy Peeve out from its new hiding place in the hood of her sweatshirt and tossing it aside as it shrieked in fear again. Noisy Peeve picked up on this new shriek sound and started scaring Fraidy Peeve with its own noises.

"Are we there yet? Are we there yet? Are we there yet?" whined Nagging Peeve as it sat atop the head of Lazy Peeve, who was currently curled up, half asleep in my lap.

Minutes later, the bus lurched to a stop and the two kids from the back skirted by, avoiding any possible contact as they gave us one last terrified glare before running for their lives. "I hope their faces get stuck that way," said Snarky Peeve, perched on my shoulder. "As if they're not weird too." I almost smiled at that, but Snarky Peeve saw it coming. "You look like a psycho when you smile. Maybe don't."

A few unsmiling minutes later, we got to our stop. "Get off now, please," said the bus driver. "Hurry. I'm late for quitting and never coming back," he added as

Lucy and I and all of our peeves exited the vehicle. The doors *swooshed* shut and the bus shifted into thunderous gear, giving Noisy Peeve a new grinding engine sound to replicate. *GRRRR-CHUNKA-CHUNKA – VRROOOOM*, it repeated as Copy Peeve freed itself of the bus grille just in time to be run over again as the bus burned rubber to get out of there.

Copy Peeve peeled itself off the pavement and reinflated with a *pop*. "They're indestructible?!" Lucy said as Copy Peeve waddled right back up to her and began repeating her words and copying her body language like it hadn't been roadkill just moments ago. I pulled out my phone and called Dad again. Still no answer. Lucy plopped down on the edge of the kerb and texted Mom before staring down the long road home to see if she would actually remember to pick us up on time for once.

"Why does she always forget us when we need her?!" Lucy complained, and then, despite her best efforts to hold it in, she sneezed again. The translucent gooey glob morphed into a furry creature that couldn't seem to remember what it was supposed to be. Its colour kept changing, as did its size and features. The only constant was the confused, totally clueless expression on its face. Forgetful Peeve. "I forgot what I was doing," it said as it clambered up Lucy's back and sat on her shoulders. It looked out like a sailor searching for land as if its purpose were somewhere just over the horizon. Lucy shoved it off and yelled, "You were getting away from me!" Forgetful Peeve nodded in agreement and started to wander off, but after a few steps seemed to forget where it was going and turned round to climb right back up on to Lucy's shoulders again.

Copy Peeve had just started mirroring Lucy's defeated slump when a Jeep Cherokee came skidding up, running over Copy Peeve and squishing it into the pavement with a sound like a Go-Gurt packet exploding. It was Dad. He was in a rush, again. He rolled down his window just low enough to yell out, "Get in!" Lucy jumped into the front seat, eager to get away from her peeves. I followed her, a step behind. Lazy Peeve clung to my backpack as if for dear life, slowing me down and giving the rest of the peeves just enough time to get into the car as well. As I climbed into the backseat, Forgetful Peeve thought to whisper to Lucy, "Sorry. I forgot what you told me to do."

The car pulled away, making an odd thumping sound that could only be Copy Peeve stuck to the front wheel. "Dad! We've been calling and texting like crazy! Why weren't you answering?!" I shouted.

"I was in meetings – and it's supposed to be your mother's day," he responded in an exasperated tone. "But she's apparently not feeling well and doesn't want to expose you to it. So I had to leave work to come and get you just to go right back to work again – which is just so typical."

"Good!" I responded. "We need to go back to Clarity Labs!"

But Dad skimmed right past that, distracted by the thumping sound outside. "What is that sound? Is that a flat tyre?" asked Dad. "Just what I need now." He was about to pull over when Copy Peeve was flung up against Lucy's window, sticking to it like a double-headed dead bug. The thumping tyre sound ended, and Dad pulled back onto the road, relieved. But now Lucy had Copy Peeve stuck to her window. And more important, she was completely fed up.

"Dad, PVZ is contagious!" Lucy shouted, with Copy Peeve shouting the same thing twice outside the window.

Dad rolled his eyes and sighed. "A treatment can't be contagious, honey."

Lucy rolled the window down, hoping to peel Copy Peeve off, but Copy Peeve just flopped onto her lap, reinflating and sitting next to her instead, totally

proving Dad wrong. Except Dad couldn't see it. "What do you even know about PVZ anyway?" he asked.

"It makes you sneeze out these little monsters that mock all your worst anxieties and insecurities!" I exclaimed, temporarily forgetting how crazy this would sound to someone who can't see them. "And they're contagious!"

"Did your mom take you to see *Gremlins* at the Vintage? She knew that was gonna be our thing!" he said, totally missing the point.

"No, Dad! Something happened yesterday. While you were in your focus group," I said. "There was . . . an accident." Dad's eyes shot up at me in the rear-view mirror. "What accident?!" he shout-asked.

I was about to confess to the whole episode when Lucy cut me off to say, "This old guy dropped a bottle of PVZ and it shot all over Slim!"

"It did?" Dad replied. "Seriously? Why didn't you tell me?"

"We didn't want to get in trouble," I offered as Noisy Peeve made all sorts of *VROOM BEEP SWOOSH SIGH CRASHING* noises, Sniffle Peeve snorted phlegm, Lazy Peeve snored and Crazy Peeve squished my face around like Play-Doh. "But now we're infected," I added.

Dad sighed and said, "You're not in trouble and you're not infected." Then he finally looked up at me in the rear-view mirror and was startled by the expression Crazy Peeve had me making. "But you're definitely letting your imaginations run wild," he added in that awful, holier-than-thou tone that parents take when they don't want to engage in a conversation.

Lucy looked back at me in frustration. But just as I managed to get Crazy Peeve off my face, Telling Peeve began spilling more of my internal thoughts. And now that Lucy could hear it, my secret was out. "He hides the Twizzlers in his safe space."

"What safe space? Where is it?" she asked instinctively.

But instead of answering her, Telling Peeve pointed at me and blurted out, "He takes super long showers because he really likes to wash his—" I covered its mouth before it could finish the sentence, but of course Snarky Peeve chimed in, "If he keeps going to the closet with Suzie, it'll have to be a lot of cold showers from now on."

Lucy was now sufficiently grossed out and I was now sufficiently humiliated. "Oh my God, I really didn't want to know any of that," she said, turning back to the front.

"What? What don't you want to know?" asked Dad, totally confused because, of course, he hadn't heard anything Telling Peeve had said.

When I let go of Telling Peeve, it blurted out as fast as it could talk, "He hates himself. He thinks he's bad. He thinks he bothers everyone and ruins everything and no one likes him and he's never going to be normal and—" I covered its mouth again, horrified that it was exposing my innermost thoughts.

"Are peeves bad too? Is that what we are? Are we bad?" wondered Asking Peeve. The little creature looked genuinely concerned, but I was so aggravated that I couldn't help but shout, "Yes, you're bad!" really loud.

Asking Peeve shrank back. I'd hurt its feelings. But Dad looked in the rear-view mirror again and said, "Hey, now. Don't talk to your sister like that."

But Lucy interrupted him. She knew I wasn't yelling at her and had to get him to understand that we really needed help. "What's Plum Island?" she asked.

"It's . . . across the sound from us. It's where that ferry by the labs goes," came Dad's confused reaction to the abrupt change of topic. "Why do you suddenly care about that?"

"I heard your boss lady mention it," Lucy replied

just as Fraidy Peeve finally peeked out of its hiding place in her hood. "She said, 'If the FDA starts poking around, we won't survive Plum Island.'" Fraidy Peeve saw itself in the side-view mirror at the exact moment Lucy said "Plum Island" again and frightened itself right back into hiding.

Dad looked up at the rear-view mirror just as Crazy Peeve returned to squishing my face around. He must have thought I was making insane faces myself because Dad then leaned over to Lucy and whispered, "Stop getting him worked up over this nonsense. You know he's sensitive!"

Lucy slumped down in her seat and sulked the way she does when no one is paying attention to her. It really bugs her – and now Dad was totally doing it to her again. So it was no surprise when she sneezed out Ignoring Peeve, which started as a translucent glob of goo on the dashboard and immediately blended into the leathery surface as if it were camouflaging itself. The only way we knew that it hadn't just disappeared was its eyes, which instantly looked away from Lucy as soon as she made eye contact. "Great. I get the ones that forget and ignore me. Just like real life," she said – an accusation that Ignoring Peeve ignored.

"Wanna trade?" was the best I could offer as my peeves hounded me.

Dad's phone rang through the dashboard Bluetooth. It was Mom calling. Noisy Peeve instantly repeated the alert while Dad answered on speakerphone. Mom sounded really weird. "Dale! Are you there yet? Are the kids . . . okay?"

Asking Peeve turned to me and asked, "Are you okay?"

"Not even close," I told it, and Mom, but she didn't hear me.

"We're fine, Leslie. On our way back to work. How are you feeling? Is this gonna be a twenty-four-hour sort of bug that magically disappears when it's more convenient for you?" he asked.

"Bug? What? How did you . . . Oh. Um. I don't know . . . what . . . it is." Mom sounded really distracted and a bit frazzled. "Maybe you should keep the kids tonight."

Dad knew her well enough to tell that something wasn't right. "What's going on, Leslie? Do you have the flu or something?"

But Mom didn't answer. Instead, we heard the sound of her pulling the phone away and saying, "I know, I know, I'll do it, I'll get to it," in an urgent whisper to someone who wasn't us before replying to Dad. "I have . . . something. Yeah. Just, um . . . yeah, if you could take care of Slim and Lucy tonight . . ."

The speakerphone said, "Call ended." We sat there in silence for a beat — at least we humans did. Crazy Peeve was going nuts, bouncing around and making gibberish noises. Suddenly Lucy swatted it out of the way. "Peeves," she said to me as an explanation for what was happening with Mom.

Dad was too confused by Mom's strange behaviour to pay attention to us, but he sure did grab our attention when he pulled a sudden U-turn, splatting all the peeves against the passenger side windows.

Five minutes later, we pulled into the driveway of the model home. The peeves were already re-forming and annoying us again. But then Dad hit the brakes so hard that the peeves splatted against the windshield. Dad sat there for a moment as Lucy unbuckled her seat belt to get out. But before she could escape, Dad grabbed her arm and looked back at me with concern. "Lucy, stay with your brother."

"Why are you always so worried about—" But before she could finish, Lucy sneezed again, right in Dad's face. He wiped the snot off, flicking the drops of translucent goo onto the gearshift. "That was really rude, Lucy," said Dad. "That's how actual disease is spread."

Meanwhile, all the droplets came together to form yet another peeve. This one really looked like it had gone through the wringer – it had almost no fur, just little patches of it here and there, and its eyes were nearly popping out of its head, with tired bags underneath that made it look almost like it'd been beaten up by its own exhaustion, and its whole body shivered with nerves. "Stay with your brother. Keep him safe. Don't let anything happen to him," said Worry Peeve in a dramatic, quavering voice. That was all I could take. I hopped out of the car as Worry Peeve called out, "I don't think he should do that!"

I ran to the house, with Lucy and my peeves and her peeves trailing close behind. We burst in through the front door like the strangest, saddest group of superheroes ever. What we found was shocking. The house Mom normally kept perfectly neat was a total disaster. Files and blueprints and calendars and schedules were all over the floor. Laundry was still sopping wet and sitting in piles on the living-room furniture. It looked like she'd been trying to make cupcakes for some reason, but the batter was half prepped and there was frosting on every surface.

Alarms and alerts were going off from every clock, phone and tablet in the house. "If this is a model home, I'd hate to see what a normal one looks like," said Snarky Peeve.

Dad caught up and pulled us behind him just as Mom hurried into the room, too busy poring over papers and shouting into her hands-free headset to even notice us. It sounded like she was trying to figure out what was going wrong with one of her renovations. It wasn't until she turned round that I realised that she wasn't actually on the phone; she was fighting with Deadline Peeve, a hyper-alert, serious-faced fur ball that was constantly looking at its wrist as if there were a watch there. It hopped up on her shoulder the minute she stopped moving and started whispering every upcoming deadline for every project, real and imagined. "I can make it. I can! I have time," she told Deadline Peeve as she waved a sheaf of papers at it.

"What's she late for?" asked Asking Peeve.

That was actually a very good question. And Mom dropped her papers when she heard it. She stared at us for a beat, as if not quite comprehending what we were doing there. Dad stepped forward cautiously, saying, "Leslie . . . what's going on?" But Lucy and I already knew she wasn't okay: Mom had peeves! Dad just had no idea. "If you're sick, you should be resting. Not doing—" he looked around at the mess, "everything imaginable all at once."

But Mom was too busy coming to terms with all the peeves to respond. She ignored Dad and rushed over to me and Lucy and hugged us so hard. "You have them too! I thought I was losing my mind! Are you okay? What are they? Why didn't you say something?" She was asking more questions than Asking Peeve, who couldn't even get one in while she was going on and on. She pulled away and looked at me apologetically. "Is this what happened this morning? Is this what you were experiencing? All these little monsters?! I'm so sorry!"

Poor Dad was just standing there, utterly confused and helpless. To him, the whole freak-out was over absolutely nothing. If he was concerned before, now he was downright terrified. "I . . . I don't know what you're talking about, Leslie. You're all seeing . . . monsters?"

"Peeves," answered Telling Peeve as it wandered up the stairs. The same word came out of my mouth and Lucy's mouth and both of Copy Peeve's mouths.

Dad repeated it like a question "Peeves?"

But Mom got it right away. "I hate deadlines.

Deadlines are one of my peeves. Now my peeve is a real thing?" Lucy and I nodded dumbly as if all we'd wanted that day was for someone to understand. "You should have realised that hours ago," chastised Deadline Peeve. Mom slumped down on the couch but immediately screamed and jumped back up. "What is that?!" she shouted, pointing at nothing. But then that nothing moved, revealing itself to be Ignoring Peeve, who had managed to blend into our sofa.

"That's mine." Lucy sighed as Ignoring Peeve turned its back on her and blended into the fireplace.

Mom moved towards Dad, who actually stepped back as if he wanted to run away. He was horror-movie scared of us.

After a moment, he seemed to realise that there was no escape – and he went straight into problem-solver mode, herding us towards the front door. "I want us all to stay very, very calm. Something is happening to all of you. You appear to be seeing things that aren't there. It might be some form of mass delusion."

Asking Peeve interrupted to wonder, "What's mass delusion? Am I mass delusion?"

"Dad, I told you! It's the PVZ!" I said, yet again. "We need to go back to Clarity Labs so that scientist guy can fix this!"

Dad quickly nodded his head like he was finally listening to me. "Yeah, okay. Let's all get in the car and go to Clarity Labs. If anyone has an answer, Dr Zanker will. Everything will be totally, totally fine if we just stay calm."

And that's when a Twizzler hit him in the head. Then another. We looked up as Twizzlers rained down upon us. Dad and Fraidy Peeve both jumped behind the couch as if they were under heavy attack. Dad looked up to see who was throwing liquorice at him, but all he must have seen was a half-empty, floating bag of Twizzlers. The rest of us, however, could see Telling Peeve, pointing at me and saying, "He hides them in his safe space!" Dad went totally pale, mouth agape, like he'd seen a ghost. That's what happens when an invisible creature throws candy at you.

"Let's go, right now!" Dad pulled us away from the front door and pushed us through the kitchen and towards the door to the attached garage while trying to give us some cover from the flying Twizzlers that haunted the front door. It was actually kind of brave, but he didn't realise that our problems were leaving the house along with us.

In the garage, Mom instinctively went to the driver's side of her car and pulled out her keys. But

Dad got there first, reaching out for them. Lucy and I had already climbed in the back with the peeves when I saw Mom reflexively yank the keys away from Dad and reach for the door. But Dad blocked it. "Leslie, you're all sick," he pleaded. "Let me drive for once."

Mom looked like she was about to argue, but then she saw me and Lucy and the swarm of peeves in the backseat with us. She sighed and let her shoulders slump, defeated. She handed the keys over to Dad.

Once we were all "safely" in her car, Mom pulled a Twizzler out of her hair. She looked at it, then looked at Deadline Peeve, then looked at all the peeves swarming around in the backseat. Eight for me, five for Lucy, one of her own, and none for Dad, who was fumbling with his seat belt behind the wheel. Mom pointed the Twizzler at me and said, "We're going to talk about this candy later." She was still in shock and it sounded almost by rote, but I have to say, it was kind of comforting to hear Mom just being Mom for a moment.

As Dad started the car, Worry Peeve leaped onto Lucy's chest, grabbing her hoodie's drawstrings. "Slim is in trouble! You should help him! You should save him!" it shouted. Lucy grabbed the drawstrings and pulled her hood up, closing it tight over her face.

Worry Peeve dropped to her lap, pulling out some of its remaining fur in a stressful fit. And for the first time, I could sort of see what being in this family might be like for Lucy – and I felt a little bad for her.

Dad opened the garage door. "It's all okay. We're all gonna be okay," he assured us unconvincingly. "There's no such thing as invisible monsters," he insisted as he started backing the car out and his hand touched the slimy snot Sniffle Peeve had already wiped on the back of Mom's seat. He instantly yanked it away and nearly crashed us into his Jeep in the process. Asking Peeve turned to look out of the rear window as we rolled down the driveway inches from collision. It tapped me on the shoulder and pointed. I think it might have almost been too shocked to talk. It just sort of stammered until it finally choked out its question: "Is THAT mass delusion?"

CHAPTER 7

THE ORIGIN

I turned and stared, gape-mouthed, out of the car window. Our neighbours were screaming and running and getting into fights amid a plague of peeves.

"That's not mass delusion," I said. "That's peeve profusion."

Mom, Lucy and I gawked at a girl walking behind her mother, who was criticising everything she did, just like the peeve doing the same thing behind her. A boy sat in his yard in frantic turmoil as a multi-armed peeve simultaneously tickled him and gave him noogies. We all turned our attention in unison as a house window smashed. The peeve that was thrown through it splatted against a tree before re-forming with a slickety-slurp.

Kids were pointing at their peeves and pleading with their parents to see what they could not (yet) see. The boy from the bus who thought the end times were upon us chased his unruly, middle-finger-waving peeve with a Bible. The body-snatcher girl who sat next to him was being chased up a tree by a peeve that seemed to chew anything she dropped. And then there was one of Heather Hu's unnamed horde-members who was simply crying on her lawn as a sticky-looking peeve repeatedly pulled her hair.

Dad snapped us back to attention when he swerved to avoid another car that was parked half in the road, half on the sidewalk, doors open. The driver was chasing after his daughter, who was running away from a cuddly-looking Hugging Peeve. They ran right past two neighbours, whose peeves were clearly based on each other. One was short, round and had the same balding hairline as one neighbour while the other was tall, skinny and had the prominent nose and ears of the other. The humans started an actual fight over their fence while the peeves egged them on below.

As we turned the corner and passed the school, I spotted Mrs Bowers, Mr Schwartz and Ms Mayfarb fending off an entire class of peeves that looked suspiciously familiar – right down to their Pokémon backpacks and Skullcandy headphones. At least I knew I wasn't the only student who annoyed them. Principal Waters rushed out of the school, swinging his briefcase at the peeves and knocking them into the road where

Dad unknowingly ran a bunch of them over. I could hear the sickening splat and slurp. But when I turned round to see them flying out from under the car, I was amazed at how quickly they re-formed as they tumbled away, knocking over a dog walker and sending his pooches into a barking fit.

Dad couldn't help rubbernecking all the weird behaviour. I could hear him gulp as he realised that something serious was obviously happening. He just had no idea what.

We made it safely across town somehow. I could see Clarity Labs rising in the distance, and I took a moment to breathe, to allow myself to think that it all might actually be okay. And that's when I realised this was the first time in a very long time that our whole family was in the same car at the same time. If not for the peeves taking up all the space, this would have felt just like the road trips we used to take up to Big Moose Lake every summer. Right down to Dad's white-knuckled driving and Mom's micromanaging of the details. Of course, this time it wasn't her fault. Deadline Peeve was shouting "advice" at her, and Mom just wasn't doing a good job of ignoring it.

In the past, being trapped in close quarters like this would have been a recipe for disaster. Every little thing that annoyed us about each other would have been amplified. It would have eventually boiled over into fighting before it resolved itself into a miserable time. But now that those annoyances were actually sitting all around us, something felt very different. At least, it did to me. I guess maybe I was so used to living with the fact that no one else could really understand what I was going through, that it was kind of nice to know that I wasn't going through it alone any more.

We pulled into the parking lot of Clarity Labs and came to a skidding stop. Dad unbuckled his seat belt as he opened his door and said, "Let's get some answers."

We barely made it to the door before security guards wearing paper medical masks blocked our entrance. "We're on lockdown," said the male one. "No one in or out," said the female one.

"I work here," replied Dad, flashing his security card.

The guards snatched his card, looked at it, then each other. The guy pressed an exterior intercom and spoke quietly into it. After an unintelligible response, he turned back to us and said, "They're waiting for you, Mr Pickings," as if we had been expected all along. They slapped paper masks on our faces and the female guard escorted us across the lobby and all the way to the doors Lucy had sneaked through yesterday, swiping us into the restricted lab section. I was the last one through, thanks to the weight of Lazy Peeve, currently forcing me to carry it piggyback-style.

The security guard led us down the metallic echo chamber of a hallway. Sniffle Peeve's slimy snorts became a surround-sound gag fest. And Noisy Peeve was having a field day with all the squeaking sounds and echoes we were making. We passed the room where this all began and Lucy pointed it out to Mom, whispering, "That's where they keep the PVZ-infected lab rats!" Which caused Fraidy Peeve to burrow deeper into her hood as Copy Peeve repeated her words and then repeated the echo of its repeat of her words and then repeated the echo of the echo of that echo. It was enough to make my head spin.

"What's a lab rat?" asked Asking Peeve.

"That is," said Telling Peeve, pointing at me. "And that, and that, and that . . ." it said, pointing at the rest of my family.

"Well, if they aren't yet, they will be soon," added Snarky Peeve, eyeing the glass-enclosed exam rooms we were passing.

"What's going to happen to him?" said Worry Peeve

in trembling apprehension, pulling on Lucy's jeans and motioning to me as if I were the only one in trouble.

Lucy sighed in frustration. "You're *my* peeve. Why are you only worried about *him*?!" Forgetful Peeve suddenly remembered it belonged to Lucy and shuffled over to her, while Ignoring Peeve did not. It just blended into the metallic hallway like it wasn't even there. It was quickly becoming my favourite of the peeves, I have to say.

The room we were put in was "hermetically sealed". I'm not sure what that means, but I knew we couldn't get in or out without a security card. The guard said it was for our own protection before slipping out and sealing the doors shut behind her. There were no windows, just a big metal wall on one side and thick glass walls on the others. Through one of them we could see an attached room with all sorts of monitors. There were a couple of exam tables, a lot of high-tech-looking lab tools I'd never seen before, and security cameras in every corner of the ceiling. One machine kept making a sound like a photocopier, and Noisy Peeve bellowed its bullfrog throat, happily mimicking it. "I want to go. Are we done yet? I don't like it here," said Nagging Peeve. And I felt the same way. Even though we came here voluntarily, I was definitely starting to feel like we were being forcibly detained.

Lab technicians huddled in the connected room, watching and whispering to each other, but we couldn't hear what they were saying. All we could hear was Mom's Deadline Peeve prattling on and on: "The fumigators are at the site. You have to pay the electricity bill. The PTA bake sale is tomorrow and you ran out of ingredients for gluten-free, sugar-free, dairy-free, nut-free cupcakes!" Mom looked totally frazzled and suddenly screamed, "SHUT UP SHUT UP SHUT UP!" Dad ran over to her, still so confused as to what was happening.

"Leslie . . . you're scaring the kids," he said in a hushed manner. But Lucy and I exchanged a look, confirming that it was him, and not us, that she was actually scaring.

"How are *you* NOT hearing this? We're surrounded!" she shouted before smoothing her hair and walking away from him and Deadline Peeve.

The doors slid open and Dr Zanker finally arrived, all twitchy and rumpled and wearing a surgical mask. "That's the guy!" I said. "He dropped the PVZ!"

Dad walked up to him the same way he'd approach my baseball coach after every time I struck out or sat down in the outfield to pick at the grass. "Dr Zanker. What is going on? What's happening to them?" he asked, gently but firmly, gesturing to us. Mom was muttering about her schedule to Deadline Peeve, Lucy was repeatedly kicking her peeves and splatting them against the glass walls, and Crazy Peeve was once again using my face like Play-Doh, causing me to make the weirdest expressions. Even I knew we all looked insane.

"Your son and I had a little run-in yesterday," said Dr Zanker as he approached me. "He was exposed to a rather large dose of PVZ." He looked at me like the prize at the bottom of a cereal box. "Tell me how you're feeling."

"He says he's seeing things!" Dad answered. "They all are!"

Dr Zanker shot Dad a frustrated look. "Mr Pickings, I'm here to help. Please allow me to examine your family," he said in a serious tone that I think he meant to be soothing but actually creeped me out. "It's the only way to figure out what's really happening to them," he continued. Even though I couldn't see his mouth, I could tell he was smiling. He was actually excited about all of this.

He summoned a pair of lab technicians into the

room to examine Mom and Lucy. And as he checked my vital signs and took a blood sample, I told him all about the series of events that led to this moment. Dr Zanker listened and nodded and made "interested" noises that Noisy Peeve immediately imitated as Worry Peeve hassled Lucy about whether I was going to be okay. Dr Zanker then stepped back to get a good, thoughtful look at my whole being and spoke into a digital recording device. "Patient Zero shows signs of agitation, possible hallucinations and delusional behaviour," he said. I've heard the term "Patient Zero" used in zombie movies and stuff, but I had never heard someone say it in real life. And I definitely didn't like that it was being used to describe me. But I was the first to be exposed to PVZ, so I guess I am "Patient Zero". I've definitely been called worse.

"What is Patient Zero? Are you sick? Am I sick?" asked Asking Peeve in response.

And without thinking, I responded to it. "I'm Patient Zero. I might be sick. And you might be the sick that's making me sick."

Dr Zanker was surprised, lifting his recording device again. "Patient Zero is communicating with his own hallucinations."

That's when I started pointing out all the peeves in

the room that he couldn't see. "I'm not hallucinating. I'm talking to Asking Peeve. It asks questions. All the time. And there's Telling Peeve and Snarky Peeve and Lazy Peeve and Crazy Peeve and Nagging Peeve and Noisy Peeve and Sniffle Peeve, which is why my sleeve is covered in snot, and those are just the ones that belong to me. Mom's got Deadline Peeve and Lucy has Copy Peeve and Fraidy Peeve and Forgetful Peeve and Worry Peeve and Ignoring Peeve – and the whole town is covered in all sorts of other ones!" I finished in one panicked breath.

"You named them all?" asked Mom in surprise.

Dad stared, gape-mouthed, as Dr Zanker's eyes lit up as if that registered in some dark corner of his brain. He kept recording his observations: "Patient Zero claims to be interacting with physical manifestations of his own irritations. His own . . . peeves."

That's when Crazy Peeve bounced off a wall, crashing onto a table and sending syringes flying across the room. Dad ducked to avoid being impaled. "See! That happened earlier! Things are moving on their own!" he shouted.

Dr Zanker quickly stepped outside and went to the adjoining room. Through the glass partition, I could see him flip on a bank of monitors that must have been connected to the security cameras in the corners because we all showed up on screen. But the video stream went from a normal image of my family and the lab technicians to a strange rainbow of colours.

Without asking, Dad stepped next to me and explained, "That's a thermal image. It uses colours to show warm objects. See the yellows and oranges and reds – that's us. The furniture and other stuff is blue because it's cold." But the funny thing was that the humans clearly weren't the only warm things in the room. I could see the surprise on Dr Zanker's face as he noticed the heatwaves emanating from too many spots. Dad's face dropped as well as he made the very same realisation. There were more living things in the room than they could see with their eyes. Which proved the peeves were real! And they could see them now – sort of.

Dad grabbed me, trying to pull me away from the invisible monsters as Dr Zanker rushed back into the room, practically bursting with excitement. He waved his arms through empty space hoping that he could touch the peeves even if he couldn't see them. "Are they over here? Is it Asking Peeve? Where is it, exactly? Hello . . . Asking Peeve?" he said, calling out to the peeves.

"What's wrong with him?" asked Asking Peeve.

"What's right with him?" responded Snarky Peeve.

But Dad was fed up. "My family is not some sort of experiment. For God's sake, Zanker, I thought PVZ was just an anti-anxiety treatment! It's all natural!"

"The 'all' part of 'all natural' may be slightly exaggerated," replied Dr Zanker.

Mom and Lucy were still being poked and prodded by the lab technicians – *lift that arm, cough, bend this way, make a fist, open up* – and their persistence eventually got the better of my mom and sister. At exactly the same time, they yelled at the technicians, "Stop bossing us around!" It was like a perfect two-note harmony, high and low, mother and daughter, indistinguishable but for their pitch. And it was followed by a synchronised sneeze. Mom, Lucy, and I stared at the floor while Dad and Dr Zanker looked over at the thermal image screens as the pair of sneezes became an identical pair of Bossy Peeves, right down to the pinstriped fur and chest-length dark patch that looked kind of like a power tie.

The Bossy Peeves instantly put their paws on their hips and started telling everyone what to do. "That doesn't go there. Tuck your shirt in. Stand up straight," said one, only to be contradicted by the other. "Leave that there. Untuck your shirt. Slouch down more." When they heard each other trying to be the boss, they started trying to tell each other what to do, since only one of them could actually be in charge.

"I'm the boss."

"No, I'm the boss."

"You do what I say."

"No, you do what I say."

It would have been funny if it hadn't been so weird. Dr Zanker ran over, examining the area of the sneezes in hopes of seeing something he still couldn't see without thermal imaging. "I'm Dr Zanker," he said excitedly, extending a hand as if to shake. "What kind of peeve are you?" But the Bossy Peeves had moved and Dr Zanker looked pretty stupid shaking hands with an empty space.

"Where do we *really* come from?" asked Asking Peeve like a little kid wanting to know how babies are born. "Do we exist before you sneeze?"

That was a heavy question from a little peeve, but it made me realise that there was something kind of cute about the little fur ball and its persistent curiosity. Everything was infinitely interesting to Asking Peeve. The world was a wonderful mystery. I spent so much time just trying to get through the day that that kind of earnestness usually bugged the bejesus out of me. But for better or worse, Asking Peeve noticed everything and wanted to know more about it – and I kind of respected it for that.

I wasn't sure where peeves really came from, but Lucy cut in with her theory: "Plum Island! Right, Dr Zanker?"

Before Dr Zanker could respond, the doors opened with a *whoosh*, followed, as always, by Noisy Peeve imitating the sound. Pauline Salt's heels *click-clacked* as she entered the room like a bird of prey in a surgical mask, which she somehow rocked like a fashion accessory. She looked at Dad and said, "Dale, I'm so sorry about this very unfortunate situation." Then without a beat, she turned on Dr Zanker and said, "There are reports of an outbreak of 'mass hysteria' in town. We need to make sure Clarity Labs is clear of any culpability."

She stared at us as if we were simply products gone wrong. "This is a PR nightmare. Who's to say that this is even our fault?" she added, as if we were at a press conference. But her statement fell flat in front of this particular audience.

Dr Zanker was still fully enamoured with his own accidental discovery. "Science is a fickle thing," he mumbled as he kept trying to make physical contact with the peeves that he didn't realise were actively avoiding him. "One wrong move and the outcome can be the opposite of what you intended," he continued. "Especially when you alter an experiment's original intention," he added, almost as if he forgot anyone else could hear him.

But Dad heard him loud and clear and was not happy. "What, exactly, was PVZ originally intended to do, Zanker?"

Pauline Salt stepped between them and warned Dr Zanker, "Say one word and you will be violating your confidentiality agreement."

But Dr Zanker scoffed. "Ms Salt, this may not be what you had planned when you engaged my services for Project PVZ, but it's a scientific breakthrough nonetheless. I've created life!" He motioned all around us at the peeves that neither he, nor Ms Salt, could currently see. That is, until she caught sight of the monitors in the other room and noticed all the little warm bodies around her feet. She *click-clacked* away as Dr Zanker exclaimed, "We can't hide progress!"

She looked at him like he'd lost his mind.

And that's when Dad completely lost his patience and did something very un-Dad-like. He slammed Dr Zanker against a wall. "WHAT WAS IT MEANT TO DO?!" He was practically choking the scientist with his lab coat as if he were determined to shake the cure out of him.

"Top . . . secret," was all Dr Zanker could squeak out.

Dad slammed him again, choking him harder. "What's on Plum Island?!"

Dr Zanker was flailing, clearly not used to fighting. A couple more slams and he looked like he was finally scared enough to give a straight answer. "Animal Disease Centre. Military Division. Lab 257," he confessed.

"THAT'S ENOUGH!" shouted Pauline Salt. "Dale, let him go. You don't want me to file an HR report."

Dad looked at her like she was certifiable for thinking that an HR report was a genuine concern of his at the moment. "Military?" he asked. "Was PVZ . . . a weapon?!"

"What it may or may not have been has no bearing on what it is now," she rationalised. "Products evolve for better uses."

Asking Peeve tugged on my sleeve and asked, "What's a weapon?"

"Something meant to hurt people," I answered, still stunned at this revelation.

"Do I . . . hurt people?" asked a trembling Asking

Peeve. And I totally got what it was worried about. My existence had only ever caused problems for everyone around me. But it wasn't Asking Peeve's fault it was born this way. And in the moment, I thought for the first time maybe it's not mine either.

"No. You're actually kind of useful. Sometimes you ask good questions," I told it.

Asking Peeve perked up, looking almost proud for a moment. But then it got confused again. "How do I know when it's a good question?"

"That's something I ask myself a lot," I replied. "It actually drives me . . ." I trailed off, looking around at all the peeves, relentlessly peeving. "Crazy," I finished. And I looked at Dr Zanker with a sudden realisation. "PVZ was originally meant to drive people crazy, wasn't it?"

Dr Zanker looked almost impressed with my deduction, but said nothing. That is, until Dad slammed another response out of him. "Biological warfare is complicated!" Zanker squealed. "And apparently the consumer-facing application is not quite ready for market."

Dad dropped Dr Zanker to the ground and shot an appalled look at Pauline Salt. She smiled and held her head high and kept her back straight as if she thought she could stonewall us until we agreed that nothing was really wrong. "You let me develop an ad campaign for a former biological weapon?!" Dad shout-asked.

But Pauline Salt didn't flinch at the question. She didn't react at all. It was like she already knew how to spin this. "When you really think about it, aren't all medications a form of biological warfare?" Dr Zanker nodded his full agreement, but the rest of us were dumbfounded that she could defend any of this. "We'll do whatever we can to remedy the situation for you and your family," Pauline Salt assured Dad, "but I need you to work with us. There might be a real opportunity here. We could make our other anti-psychotic medications available to the public. Clarity Labs could come out of this as the heroes that rescued this town from an outbreak."

The vein in Dad's forehead looked like it was going to pop. I thought he was about to have a coronary. Instead, he sneezed. And there, right at his feet, his very own peeve was forming. And with its fur smoothed into crisp, clean lines and its angular, uppity face that seemed to be carved into a permanent scowl, it looked an awful lot like Pauline Salt. "Save the company. Spin that story. Drug the masses," Salty Peeve said just before it *click-clacked* across the room and started arguing with the two Bossy Peeves that thought they were in charge here. Dad looked at his very first peeve. Then he looked around the room at all the other peeves he could suddenly see for the first time. He took a deep breath and nodded his head. I think he might have actually been relieved.

"Oh . . . okay. I get it now," he said.

But it was Mom's turn to interrogate Pauline Salt. "Why did you hire a biological weapons creator to make medicine? How is that ethical? What is going to happen to us now? Is this going to get worse? And which dry cleaner will you use when I sue you so hard you poop that pretty white suit of yours?!" she shouted, but she used Dad's word for poop. And I'm glad she did.

Dad grabbed her arm and pulled her back before she could haul off and slug Pauline Salt, but she did manage to yank the mask off her face, causing Ms Salt to cover her mouth and nose in an uncharacteristic panic. But then, in a disturbingly calm tone, Dad told Dr Zanker, "You'll give us the cure for this condition. Right. Now."

Dr Zanker began to respond, but then stopped himself. Instead of what he was originally going to say, he gave Dad a shifty look and simply stated, "PVZ was meant to BE the cure."

And at that moment, the fire alarms went off – again. Through the glass doors we could see lab technicians and other employees running down the hall outside as if in panic. I looked accusingly at Lucy, but she swore, "It wasn't me this time."

Pauline Salt and Dr Zanker peered through the glass doors, confused, but the rest of us could see what was happening just fine. "Clarity Labs has peeves," said Dad.

We could hear screaming and glass breaking as the fire sprinklers in the hall clicked on to put out a fire caused by a scorched, flaming-red Pyro Peeve that anyone who wasn't peeve-infected couldn't see. Pauline Salt rushed out of the room to handle the emergency, leaving the rest of us staring at Dr Zanker, lost in his own thoughts. He lifted his digital recorder again, talking as if no one could hear him. "It must have been the original amoebas. Something in the genetic code," he said, peering at my head so intensely it was like he was trying to see through it. "They were only single cells, but they were alive."

"What are you talking about?" I said, backing away from him.

"But if PVZ has reverted to its original state," he continued as if I were just a rat that had squeaked at him, "and it has evolved into independent organisms separate from their hosts . . . will it continue to follow the original stages of weaponised PVZ? And what form would those stages take?"

"STAGES?! What stages?" I practically shouted. "Are these peeves going to . . . EVOLVE?!"

Dr Zanker snapped out of his reverie, as if he were surprised to have actually said that out loud. But he smiled, creepily, not caring. "That's what irritations do when left unchecked," he said as he backed towards the door. "I just need to watch you carefully to track their progress."

That gave Dad a sudden realisation of his own: "You're not going to help us."

"We can help each other," replied Dr Zanker as he swiped himself through the doors. "At my *real* lab. Away from these ridiculous corporate restraints."

"We're not your lab rats!" shouted Mom as Dr Zanker swiped his security card again, sealing the doors between us.

"Then why are you in a cage?" he asked as he hurried to the adjacent room, ignoring the peeve-related chaos around him. We all pounded on the doors, trying to get them open, but it was no use. Dad searched his pockets and then cursed himself, remembering, "The guard has my security card!"

"No, she doesn't," admitted Lucy as she handed the card to him. Mom and Dad exchanged a surprised look, unsure how Lucy got her hands on it. But I just smirked at her, impressed that her "borrowing" habit had actually come in handy for a change.

Dad swiped the card, opened the doors and guided us all out.

"But what do we do about him?" asked Asking Peeve. It was pointing at Dr Zanker, who saw our escape and came rushing out of the adjacent room in pursuit. Thinking fast, I grabbed Sniffle Peeve and smeared its face across the hallway behind us as we fled.

Dr Zanker slipped on the trail of snot left behind and landed hard on his back. Sniffle Peeve gave me a proud little sniffle for finally being useful for something. And the last thing I saw before we turned the corner was a scary-looking Jokey Peeve with a clown nose yanking off Dr Zanker's surgical mask, honking his nose, and bouncing away.

As we hurried down the hall, I heard Dad tell Lucy, "I'm sorry I didn't listen to you."

Lucy briefly smiled. "Sometimes it's hard to separate the nonsense from the makes sense." But her smile faded as we entered a lobby that was swarming with peeves. They were at the front desk, tangling receptionists in phone cords as the phones rang off the hook. They were chasing and tackling and tormenting employees who were trying to flee the building now that the security guards were hounded by their own little monsters. They were climbing the walls and tearing things down and smashing test tubes filled with chemicals that began to mix and smoke in strange colours.

"We simply must prepare a press release. We can't be blamed for this," said Salty Peeve as if it wasn't part of the problem.

A Clarity Labs employee ran right between us, knocking me over into Asking and Telling Peeves as she fought off a peeve that was giving her a massive wedgie. She knocked it off, picked up a chair, and swung it at the peeve, smashing a hole through a floor-to-ceiling window behind me.

"How far can you jump?" asked Asking Peeve.

I was confused until Telling Peeve pointed up and shouted, "It's gonna crash down on you!"

The hole in the window sent cracks all the way to the top. The upper part of the glass collapsed. I grabbed the peeves and dived away as the window shattered to the floor, scattering broken glass everywhere.

I looked at Asking and Telling Peeves, surprised and thankful for the assistance. Mom and Dad ran over to help me up and out of the door with Lucy and the rest of our peeves.

Just as we got to the car, I glanced back at Clarity Labs and saw that scorched little Pyro Peeve laughing maniacally before striking a match near a puddle of spilled chemicals. *This is not going to end well,* I thought.

If I only knew then how right I'd be.

CHAPTER 8

THE FLEEING FAMILY

Clarity Labs was barely in our rear-view mirror before my thoughts turned to Dr Zanker's comment about irritations evolving. If these little, totally annoying peeves caused this much mayhem at stage one, what terrible things could we expect next?

Dad was driving and Mom sat next to him. Deadline Peeve was standing in her lap, its finger in her face, telling her, "Stage two is coming. And then stage three is coming. But not till after stage two – and they better not be late!"

Asking Peeve turned to me, "What is stage two? What is stage three? Are there more stages after that? What happens to us when we evolve?"

"I don't know," I said. "But we have to get help. We have to talk to some actual, real, non-psychotic doctors. We need to go to the hospital!"

"I'm on it," said Dad, actually listening to me for once.

He made a hard turn, setting a new course as Mom's front seat Bossy Peeve bickered with Lucy's backseat Bossy Peeve about the best way to get there.

"Take a left."

"No, take a right and then a left."

"Now go straight."

"Turn round."

"We've got to cover our tracks. That's the most important thing," added Salty Peeve.

Mom and Dad were so thrown by the mayhem that they managed to avoid arguing with each other – at least for a few minutes. The peeves did that for them.

In the backseat, Lucy was squished in next to me and all the other peeves. She was really stressed and was really tired of Fraidy Peeve clinging to her. Noisy Peeve had stuck its head between us and was imitating a car horn that it had heard somewhere along the way. Lazy Peeve snored in my lap. I caught Lucy's eye and though she looked like she might cry, she said something I really wasn't expecting: "I'm sorry." I think I just sort of blinked at her, like I didn't quite understand the sounds her mouth was making. Luckily, Copy Peeve repeated everything she said, right down to her sincere look of regret. Twice. "If I hadn't shoved you out of the lab and into Zanker, none of this would be happening." She'd never apologised to me without Mom or Dad threatening dire consequences, so despite all the snotty little science experiments sitting between us, at that moment, Lucy's apology was the strangest thing in the car.

Once I got over the shock of it, I realised it had never crossed my mind that this was anyone's fault. I was so used to dealing with my own problems that I really wasn't in the habit of looking for people to blame. Sure, Lucy drove me crazy, but I always thought being driven crazy was just part of what was wrong with me.

"He's oversensitive, excitable and anxious," Telling Peeve blurted out.

"That's an understatement," interrupted Snarky Peeve.

"He thinks it's all his fault," Telling Peeve let Lucy know. She looked at me in a way I couldn't quite describe – like she could actually relate to me for once. She even put a hand on my shoulder and gave it a gentle squeeze.

So of course, that's when Noisy Peeve let out a fart noise.

The sound brought us right back to reality: Mom and Dad (and their peeves) were arguing in the front and it was hard to even know who was saying what:

"The hospital is that way!"

"I know where it is."

"Then why are you going this way?"

"Which way would you like me to go?"

"The fastest way to the hospital!"

"That's exactly where I'm going!"

Crazy Peeve jumped up and down on the seat between us, jabbering, "Grun grun zick zock!" but then slipped on Sniffle Peeve's snot trail and face-planted. Telling Peeve stepped on top of it as if Crazy Peeve were a podium, looked at Lucy and pointed at me. "He broke the porch swing and let you take the blame for it."

Lucy's eyes lit up. "I KNEW IT!"

Round the curve into the heart of Old Wayford, the traffic bottlenecked and Dad had to slam on the brakes to avoid an accident, which sent all of our unbuckled peeves flying against the windshield and seat backs. "You've got to be kidding me with this traffic!" shouted Dad. Then he sneezed. Judging by the way the ensuing peeve had three eyes that flashed like a broken stoplight and was instantly getting in his way and blocking his view, I had to assume it was Traffic Peeve.

As the peeves peeled themselves off the windshield

and started to scuttle back to join the others reinflating in the backseat, Traffic Peeve did its best to get in their way too. Noisy Peeve started making the car horn sounds from outside. And Forgetful Peeve stayed up front; it seemed to have no idea what it was supposed to be doing. I strained to see what was happening ahead of us, but Lazy Peeve climbed into my lap and fell back asleep, weighing me down again. Nagging Peeve kept tugging on my sleeve, hounding me with, "Are we there yet? Are we there yet? Are we there yet?" and Worry Peeve kept answering by saying, "He's going to be so, so, so late." For what, I don't know. Crazy Peeve zipped from seat to seat while Telling Peeve rattled off even more of my least favourite secrets. "He pees a little when he laughs too hard and when he gets really scared. He hates the road trips to Big Moose Lake. He cheated on his third grade maths test."

"And he still failed," replied Snarky Peeve.

Mom briefly turned round from the front seat. "We're going to talk about that test later!"

"Too late," noted Deadline Peeve.

"It has a point," agreed Dad, surprising us all. "We have more pressing matters to deal with right now. Like getting some actual help."

That's when I became aware of Asking Peeve,

sitting next to me, quietly wondering out loud: "What's the point? Why are we even here? Can anyone really change?"

Lucy looked down at Asking Peeve, then up at me as if I were the one asking the questions. "Is this what it's like for you all the time? How do you deal with it?"

I was so startled that I didn't really know what to say. No one has ever been able to actually see my problems. Even before the peeves were here, a lot of things drove me crazy, so I guess I had sort of built up what my therapist called "coping skills". In fact, compared to people who don't have as many anxieties as I do, my therapist told me my tolerance levels were practically superhuman. Then again, my annoyance levels were also superhuman, so it made sense that I'd have to be that much better at coping. Not that anyone else ever saw it that way. My meltdowns made it seem like I was actually so much worse at dealing with things than everyone else. But maybe my therapist was right. Maybe I was actually really good at dealing with my problems. Everyone else's peeves were driving them crazy, but at this point, I had started to see some of my peeves as, well, almost useful.

Copy Peeve repeated Lucy's question: "How do you deal with it?" Twice.

But then Asking Peeve asked an even better question: "Does he have the option to NOT deal with it?"

"Exactly!" I said to Asking Peeve, who smiled at me as if it were starting to understand. But there wasn't time to answer either question because we had finally entered town – and what was happening inside the car was nothing compared to what was happening outside it.

CHAPTER 9

THE EVOLUTION

Dad pulled the car to a stop in the middle of town. He didn't have a choice: cars were abandoned all over the road and there was no way to get round them. He put the car in reverse and tried to back up, but bumped right into another car blocking our way.

"So much for going to the hospital," said Lucy. She was right. The hospital was a whole town over, and we were clearly not going anywhere far anytime soon.

People were running all over the place, swarmed by masses of peeves. Cars were wrecked, fires were breaking out and a hydrant was spraying water into the street as people were desperately trying to escape or eliminate their peeves. They were squishing them under cars, flattening them with sledgehammers, chasing them with blowtorches and axes, and I even heard a gunshot go off. But no matter what they did, the peeves would just stretch, splat, peel, reinflate and go right back to annoying them. It was like a movie version of the zombie apocalypse, except instead of the undead, the townsfolk were being hounded by furry little creatures.

The peeves inside the car started going even more bonkers upon seeing what was happening outside. Dad clicked the locks down, sealing us in the car. He was dumbstruck. "It's like . . ."

But I finished the thought for him: ". . . every day inside my head." My whole family turned to look at me. I hadn't realised I'd said it out loud, but Lucy was right. This is what it's like for me every day. A relentless barrage of clashing, crashing, irrational feelings, irritations and anxieties that never leave me alone. And for a brief moment, they didn't look at me the way they usually do. The fear and frustration and concern and confusion were replaced by a sort of brokenhearted look of understanding. Like they finally got it: this was the living embodiment of the thought spirals I navigate just to function every day. Mom teared up; she could only muster an "Oh, sweetie . . ." as Dad reached back and put his hand on my knee and gave it a squeeze. And Lucy didn't say a thing, which was about the nicest thing she could do. All that love and goodwill coming at me at once was actually making me squirm.

And then: SLAM!

We all jumped in our seats as a man ran smack into the side of our car, knocking himself out cold. His peeves swarmed over him and jumped up and down on his prone body until he came to, staggered to his feet, and ran away with his peeves clinging to him wherever they could get a handhold.

"There must be a way to kill these things," Dad said.

"Do it. Do it now," Mom's Bossy Peeve ordered, pointing at Lucy's Bossy Peeve. But Dad grabbed the first one by the throat and tried to choke it to death. Its head and body squished around every time he squeezed, like a water balloon that was only half full. "You're doing it wrong. Try it sideways," demanded Lucy's Bossy Peeve, hoping to eliminate its competition.

"We could make a run for it. Maybe if we get far enough away from here the peeves will wear off?" Mom suggested as a woman ran past while being berated by an orange peeve with tiny paws and an unruly tuft of yellow hair on its head. It was shouting a whole lot of nasty comments I shouldn't repeat while trying to pull her hijab off. Lucky for her, that hateful little monster got hit by a taco truck and knocked into a unisex portaloo that had somehow caught fire near a section of road that was being repaved.

"They're contagious!" replied Dad as he hurled

Mom's Bossy Peeve against the back window, splatting it like one of those tacky suction-cup stuffed animals. "We can't run away from them! They'll come with us no matter where we go. A change of scenery and new coat of paint isn't the answer to everything."

"You're right, Dale. Maybe you should just offer child support to these little monsters and wash your hands of it all," she shot back. "I'm sure the problem will take care of itself."

Suddenly the fight wasn't just about what was happening with the peeves; it was about what was happening with our family. Asking Peeve asked me sadly, quietly, "Why do they want to get rid of us?"

My parents barely heard it, but Lucy and I both looked down at the little guy. After months of being bounced from parent to parent, we both knew that feeling all too well.

"He blames himself for the divorce!" Telling Peeve decided to announce.

Everything got really quiet really fast. Dad turned round and insisted, "That's just not true."

"We told you both, the split had nothing to do with either of you," continued Mom.

"I know," I said, but what I couldn't bring myself to add was that it didn't change the way I felt.

144

"Well, the peeves are definitely our fault," said Lucy.

"She's right," I added. "And if we don't deal with them here and now, they're just gonna get worse and follow us around for ever." Lucy threw me a confident nod. We were a united front for once. Maybe things could change; maybe after we got rid of the peeves, things could get better. That's when my eyes were drawn beyond her, out of the window, across the square, and over to the pharmacy where we always pick up my prescriptions. An idea hit. "If some of those medications helped calm me down, maybe they'd work on the peeves too," I suggested.

And that's when I sneezed again. But this time, I didn't sneeze out another peeve. This time a large glob of black goo shot out of my nose. And, man, did it feel weird – like it had been pulled straight out of my brain. For a moment, I felt disorientated, sort of dizzy, sort of blurry, but when everything came into focus, I realised all of my peeves were staring at the dark snot glob that was stuck to the back of Dad's seat. And unlike the translucent goo that created the peeves, this glob was pitch-black. Everyone else's peeves kept chattering away, but all of mine had suddenly calmed down. It wasn't quite the weird, dopey daze they entered around Suzie, but something had definitely changed — and not, I thought, in a good way.

"What is that?" asked Lucy as she stared at the gross black goo. "It's . . . not like the other peeves' snot. It looks . . . evil." She pointed at it but kept a careful distance.

"I don't know," I said, but I was more interested in why my peeves had suddenly stopped trying to annoy me while everyone else's continued. Mom and Dad craned round to try to get a look at whatever new monster goo I'd just sneezed out. Suddenly something moved. Lucy screamed and leaned away, but it was just Ignoring Peeve, having blended into the seat back. "I keep forgetting that one is here!" exclaimed Lucy.

"Me too," added Forgetful Peeve.

I leaned closer and dared to poke the black goo. I had some thought about trying to flick it out of the window, but I couldn't bring myself to actually pick it up. My peeves stared at it, and then each other, and then me, like they were totally confused about what they were supposed to be doing.

"Why don't I feel connected any more?" asked Asking Peeve.

"Because we're not," answered Telling Peeve.

And that explained why I felt so disorientated this

time. "Whatever that is, I think it cleared the PVZ from my system," I said.

"PVZ *is* supposed to be temporary," Dad recalled. "It's in all the disclaimers for the advertising mock-ups."

"I think stage one might be over for me," I said with a quaver in my voice, realising that the next stages would probably be coming soon.

Worry Peeve started biting its nails like they were part of its Lunchables. "He's in danger. Something bad will happen to him. You have to help," it said to Lucy as the last remaining tufts of hair fell off its body. She shoved it away.

"What's happening to us?" asked Asking Peeve, its voice full of uncertainty. Sniffle Peeve wiped its nose on the back of Mom's headrest and Crazy Peeve banged its head against its own reflection in the window.

My peeves were still defined by their annoying traits, but they weren't specifically trying to annoy me any more. And without the urge to directly annoy me, my peeves finally looked like what they really were: innocent little lab experiments. It took a moment to process, but when I noticed Asking Peeve was still looking up at me for an answer, I told it the only thing I could think to say: "I think you're free now."

"Then why are ours still so awful?" asked Mom as Deadline Peeve whispered in her ear, "You'll never get the cupcakes made on time." She was right. Dad was still contending with Traffic Peeve flashing its stoplight eyes in his face and Salty Peeve urging him to "spin" this situation.

"But some of mine are better too!" said Lucy, pointing at Forgetful Peeve, who was sitting quietly on the floor until pointing it out reminded it of its purpose.

"I forgot what I should do to annoy you. Can you remind me? And who are you again?"

Lucy sulked. "Never mind. It's just yours."

Outside the car, people were still running and fighting with their peeves and each other. "I was the first one exposed. If it's evolving now, then whatever stage two is . . . whatever that black goo is . . . it makes sense that I'd hit it first," I concluded. But that was little comfort when facing the unknown consequences of the next stage.

"What do I do with myself now?" asked Asking Peeve.

"I don't know what he's thinking any more," answered Telling Peeve, pointing at me out of habit.

"Judging by his face, it's probably still stupid," said Snarky Peeve. "But whatever, I'm my own peeve now."

Before any of the peeves, or the rest of us for that matter, had the chance to figure out what peeve freedom really meant, Noisy Peeve let out a fire alarm *BLARE* and pointed at the black goo. Asking Peeve stepped away from it, wanting to know, "Is it supposed to be doing that?"

The black goo had started jiggling like it was actually alive. Then it lurched suddenly, stretched its "arms", and started to grow! When the black goo developed a mouth that started expanding and making aggressive *om-nom-nom* sounds in our direction, my fight-or-flight instincts kicked in. I yelled, "Everyone out of the car!"

Dad flipped the locks up and we all scrambled out as fast as we could. Only Fraidy and Lazy Peeves stayed in the car. Lazy was too tired to move, and Fraidy was too scared to run. The black goo was now as big as the backseat. I stared in horror as a set of glowing-red, angry-looking eyes emerged above its garbage-truck-like maw, which opened wide to gobble Lazy and Fraidy Peeve up in one chomp, swallowing them whole. Three pairs of gelatinous legs sprang from its sides as it expanded, oozing into both the front and way back of the car.

We gathered on the kerb nearby, staring back at Mom's car, trying to wrap our heads round what was taking shape inside. There was no space left in there. The creature was starting to press up against the closed windows, cracking them as it grew too big to fit and then oozing out of the openings.

Suddenly the chaos we'd entered on the street didn't seem quite so bad. I'd take little peeves chasing us around over whatever this thing was any day. A gross, wet tongue unrolled from the black goo's mouth and grabbed Forgetful Peeve by the scruff of its neck. The poor little peeve had clearly forgotten to be afraid. "What was I doing again?" was the last thing it said as it was swallowed whole.

"It eats peeves!" shouted Dad. "Get rid of them!" He grabbed the closest peeve he could find – Asking Peeve – and threw it at the black goo.

And I surprised myself by shouting "NO!" I dived and intercepted Asking Peeve inches from the gaping maw of the black goo. It tried to eat me instead, but I crab-crawled backwards, away from it, and kicked the open car door closed, slamming it on the tongue and causing the black goo to *ROAR* something awful.

Mom and Dad pulled me to safety. "What are you doing?" Dad said, as incredulous about my one-handed catch, I think, as he was about the fact that I was trying to save a peeve.

"I don't think feeding the peeves to it is a good thing," I told him. Asking Peeve clung to me, as surprised that I saved its life as I was. "It only seems to get bigger and angrier with each one it eats," I added as the car started to shake and rattle with the rapid growth of the black goo inside.

"A change of scenery probably isn't a bad idea right now," quipped Mom, motioning to the pharmacy down the road with the same expression she reserved for my worst episodes. "We need something strong to stop this. And if it's made from out-of-control emotions, maybe Slim's right. Maybe we can dose it with drugs!"

The front and rear windows blew out as six rubbery, purplish-black legs burst through and planted firmly on the ground. The back four were insectlike. The front two had sticky paws. The whole package was unsettling. And as I watched this unbelievable monstrosity take shape, it felt almost familiar. "It's like when I go from being slightly annoyed about one thing to obsessively, furiously annoyed about everything," I muttered in a state of shock as the black goo stood, lifting our car off the ground like a turtle would its shell. Except this turtle outgrew its shell so quickly that the undercarriage separated from the frame.

"But what is it?!" cried Lucy as the black goo shook

the roof off like it was nothing and turned its angry eyes towards us.

"It's stage two!" I shouted as I stepped back, thinking up the only fitting word for exactly what I saw before me. "It's a . . . BUGBEAR!"

CHAPTER 10

THE TREATMENT PLAN

The bugbear was growing bigger quickly. It was only five minutes old and already taller than Dad. The black goo had stretched into a dark purplish hue that made the bugbear look sort of like a giant, gelatinous, six-legged insect – but with some random fur patches here and there. Like a gummy sweet that's fallen out of your mouth, landed on the floor, and is now inedible because it's got cat hair stuck to it. When it stepped into the light from the setting sun, I could vaguely see Lazy Peeve inside its translucent body. Asking Peeve looked up in horror at this creature and wondered, "Did I make that?"

"I think we made that together," I answered. The bugbear *roared* and kicked the car chassis out of its way, sending it flying into a line of cars abandoned nearby. That's when Mom and Dad grabbed us and we took off running through the town square.

But the bugbear gave chase, knocking cars out of

the way, sending townsfolk and their peeves scrambling for cover. People gaped in shock and awe as the lumbering, blackish-purple beast on six legs chased my family down the middle of a crowded street.

"This way!" ordered Mom's Bossy Peeve.

"No, that way!" demanded Lucy's Bossy Peeve.

But we just headed straight for the pharmacy, past a couple of cops who were trying to get back into their police car. Their peeves had got in, locked the car from the inside, and were now playing with the cops' guns and radio. Without slowing down, I screamed to them for help, but they turned just in time to dive out of the way as the bugbear trampled their police car, pausing for the briefest of seconds to slurp up the peeves that squished out of the windows.

Noisy Peeve couldn't resist aping the *blurp boop* sound of the dying police car siren, which drew the bugbear's attention back our way. We all glared at Noisy Peeve as the bugbear gobbled down a handful of random peeves before lumbering after us again. Salty Peeve skidded to a stop, turned and pointed at the bugbear, screaming, "This is an unacceptable liability and must be covered up!" as if that would somehow prevent it from being gobbled up. It didn't.

Then Snarky Peeve paused to say, "That's what you

get for needing to have the last word," which, ironically, were its last words before it also wound up inside the jellylike body of the bugbear.

Those peeves may have been annoying, but that exchange actually bought us enough time to lose the bugbear behind a tipped-over bus. Dad's Traffic Peeve ran up ahead of us and stood in front of the pharmacy door, flashing its top red eye like a broken stoplight, but we just ran right through it, carrying it into the pharmacy. Dad instantly locked the door behind us and dropped the blinds on the front display window, but Mom toppled a shelf against the door, nearly squashing Dad in the process. "Sorry," she said, panting with adrenaline.

"No, no," Dad responded as he climbed out from underneath the shelf that had fully secured the door. "This is one time your redecorating was actually necessary."

The place looked like a riot had broken out inside. Shelves were trashed, products were all over the floor, and some loose helium balloons from the gift card section floated by, wishing us, "Get Well Soon!" The place seemed to be empty, but the soft strains of mellow rock were still pumping through the overhead speakers. I'd been here so many times and never noticed how creepy that music could be. It's all calm and relaxing, but somehow it felt like the perfect soundtrack for all the mayhem happening outside. Or maybe I've just seen too many zombie movies.

Dad dropped the blinds on the rest of the windows as Mom overturned more stacks of shelves for our protection. "Slim's in danger," said Worry Peeve, tugging on Lucy's sleeve. "He's gonna get eaten," Worry Peeve added as she shrugged it off.

Asking Peeve crawled up the shelf towards Worry Peeve and asked, "Why don't you worry about someone else for a change?"

Worry Peeve seemed genuinely confused as it replied, "Because it's always all about Slim."

I was still catching my breath, but Mom and Dad heard this and I saw them exchange a guilty look. They had no idea this was how Lucy felt.

"There's no one here," I said as I passed Sniffle Peeve having a field day in the tissue section. "How do we even get the drugs we need without a prescription?"

"We'll just 'borrow' them," answered Lucy, already behind the pharmacist's counter, rummaging through pills. Copy Peeve followed after her, doing the same thing.

Dad slid over the counter to join her. "Just to be

clear, this sort of 'borrowing' is not okay under normal circumstances," he said.

"But these are very not normal circumstances," added Mom as she joined them.

"Stop right there!" came a shout from behind her. We all jumped as the young pharmacist who usually filled my prescriptions stepped out from a back room aiming a gun at us. "We're closed! You can't just come in here and steal drugs!" he shouted from a face that looked like it had aged a decade since I last saw him. Mom and Dad moved in front of me and Lucy protectively.

"We're not stealing; we're just . . . borrowing," said Dad as he shot Lucy an uncertain look.

"You know us. The Pickings. We usually come through the drive-through window," explained Mom, pointing behind the shelves at a sliding window I forgot was back there. "You're . . . Martin, right? We're like, your best customers," she added.

"Well, he is," said Telling Peeve, pointing my way.

"And I suppose you're just here for a refill?" said Martin, with a cracked look in his eye.

"I'm actually on a medication vacation," I muttered nervously from behind Mom. Martin stared at me suspiciously, gun swaying in my direction.

"I want to leave. Can we go now? This isn't fun," said Nagging Peeve, who was tugging at the leg of my jeans. Martin swung the gun at it, suddenly noticing the peeves all around us. "They all went crazy, you know. Right here in the store. Just started yelling at nothing and knocking things over and fighting with each other. I had to lock myself in the back till they cleared out," he said in a much higher voice than I remembered. "And now you've broken in."

"Actually, the door was unlocked," corrected Lucy. Martin swung the gun at her. "But I think the sign was flipped to 'Closed!'" she added as Crazy Peeve popped out of a box of pill bottles on a shelf by his head. Startled, Martin swung the gun in its direction and Dad tackled him, knocking the shelf over and sending Crazy Peeve sprawling to the ground, shaking pill bottles like pom-poms. The Bossy Peeves shouted fighting tips to Dad as he simultaneously struggled for the gun and swatted off Traffic Peeve, who was desperately trying to get in his way. Even though Dad was older and smaller than Martin, he was fuelled by papa bear instincts and got the upper hand, ripping the gun away from him.

"I can't believe you pulled a gun on us!" Dad shouted.

"Dad," said Lucy, pointing at the gun as Copy Peeve

did the same. He looked down to see the bright red tip on the end. He was holding a plastic squirt gun.

Martin stood up, sheepishly admitting, "It's all we had in the store." That's when I saw Lucy making the strangest face, like she sucked a lemon or something. At first I thought it was just her weird reaction to the toy gun reveal, but then it hit me: the foulest stench I'd ever smelled. I covered my nose. "Oh, man, who did that?"

We all gagged and tried to breathe through our sleeves as a squat little brown peeve came out of the back room, walking around us and fanning the air behind it with a bushy tail that none of the other peeves had. "This one lady who comes in . . . she always, ALWAYS, passes gas. I'm supposed to be sensitive to her medical condition, but she just crop-dusts the whole store with no respect for the air we have to breathe," said Martin as Farting Peeve made the rounds. "She was here when everyone went crazy. And then that thing appeared while I was hiding. I thought I'd lost my mind before you all showed up. Now I don't know what's happening!"

BEEP BEEP SWOOSH CRASH BLEEP BOOP VROOM FART.

Martin jumped away from Noisy Peeve before

crashing into another shelf and knocking boxes everywhere. This dude had been through the wringer. I felt bad for him.

"Just calm down!" said Mom in the least calm manner imaginable. Her hair was all frizzed out and her eyes seemed to have lost their ability to blink. I'd never seen her look quite so unhinged before. "We've all been exposed to something in the air."

"I know, I can smell it!" Martin shouted.

"No, not that," corrected Dad. "Well, that too," he quickly realised. "But it came from a nasal spray that should clearly never hit the shelves – and now the whole town has peeves!" he shouted, motioning to our thirteen remaining peeves.

"And a bugbear," I reminded.

"Oh, right. And a bugbear! Which is much bigger and much worse. And that's why we need the drugs," he concluded, wiping sweat from his brow and rubbing his stubble with the heels of his hands like he does when he's at his wits' end. He nearly poked his eye out with the squirt gun in the process. He tossed it away in frustration, and the Bossy Peeves immediately started fighting over it.

"Give me the gun, I'm in charge!" said Mom's Bossy Peeve.

"No, I should have it. I'm the boss," argued Lucy's Bossy Peeve.

"Where are the mood stabilisers? Anti-anxiety medication?" asked Mom.

"We need all the Xanax and Lexapro and Ritalin and Effexor and Zoloft you have!" I added. Martin, in shock at all this new information, pointed to the shelf behind us.

"What will those do?" asked Asking Peeve.

"Hopefully calm that bugbear down," I replied as we started grabbing bottles. "Results may vary. But this is one time I'm rooting for some really bad side effects."

I had just grabbed a box off a shelf and was rummaging through when I looked up to the empty space I'd left behind. There was an angry red eye staring at me. Before I could scream, the shelf was knocked over as the bugbear *roared*. Luckily for me, the shelf hit another shelf, keeping it from squashing me, but the sound of the fall knocked everyone else back a step. Pills scattered all over the floor, mixing together so we couldn't tell one type of medication from another.

I scrambled out from under the fallen shelves and we all fled towards the front counter. I figured that the bugbear must have smashed through the drive-through window during all the commotion over the squirt gun because it was still half stuck in a hole in the wall where that window used to be.

"Can we *please* go now?" came one last whine from Nagging Peeve before the bugbear's nasty tongue lashed out and snagged it, yanking it right back into its gooey mouth.

Mom and Dad and Martin tried to get the shelf Mom had knocked against the door to budge, but it was lodged too tight. "Break the window!" said both Bossy Peeves at the same time, actually making a smart demand for once. Martin grabbed a comic book rack and smashed one of the windows with it, clearing the broken blinds and glass. I was standing, frozen, staring at the angry bugbear and nervously fumbling with the childproof cap on the one bottle I was still holding.

Martin pushed ahead, leaped through the window first, and fled for his life. Mom and Dad shouted a few choice words after him before lifting Lucy through, over Traffic Peeve, who decided now was the perfect time to raise its paws and let its middle eye blink yellow. The bugbear only needed to free one more leg and it would be after me. I fumbled with the medicine bottle, my hands slick with sweat, my eyesight blurred by panic as Farting Peeve walked between us and fanned its stench up towards the bugbear. It definitely didn't like that because it let out a *ROAR* so loud that it completely drowned out the slow jams pumping through the speakers. Then it gobbled up Farting Peeve too, making a disgusted face as if it tasted as bad as it smelled. I can't say I was sad to see that one go. The bugbear kicked its final leg loose just as I popped the cap off the bottle. A few pills spilled out, but I was able to toss the rest into the bugbear's gaping mouth a moment before Dad yanked me away.

The bugbear swallowed the pills in a single gulp before lunging at us. It chomped down, barely missing my feet as we tumbled through the window and hit the sidewalk outside. We got up and ran just as the bugbear crashed through the remaining wall and continued to chase us.

Night had fallen as Mom and Dad hurried us out onto Old Wayford's Main Street, but the bugbear toppled a fire truck across the road, blocking our escape and leaving a firefighter stuck up in a tree where she was hiding from her Cat Peeve below. That role reversal came to an end when the bugbear gobbled up the Cat Peeve and knocked over the tree, blocking our next escape attempt. The firefighter lost her grip in the commotion. I thought she'd break her neck from the fall, but instead she bounced off the bugbear's gummy body, hit the ground behind it, and ran away.

I could see the bugbear had started to slow down. It wasn't stopping, but it was definitely feeling the effects of the pills. "It's working! It's calming down!" I shouted.

"But not enough," added Lucy as she pulled a couple of pill bottles from her pockets, handing one to me as we struggled to get them open.

"What's a gremlin?" asked Asking Peeve. We all looked up at the movie title pinned to the marquee of the second-run Vintage Theatre my dad and I always go to.

We were cut off from the rest of the town square by crashed vehicles and downed trees. The slower, but no less angry bugbear had us cornered. Mom and Dad pulled out the pill bottles they had and popped them open just as the bugbear charged. I grabbed Lucy and ran for the movie theater as Mom and Dad held their ground just long enough to toss their open pill bottles into the bugbear's mouth before ducking out of the way so it would clumsily crash into the fire truck.

Lucy and I ran headlong into the little movie theater that smelled of butter and first-date cologne. Mom and Dad were a step behind. They knocked over a lobby display for an animated movie that'd been out of the multiplexes for months. Mom snatched up the broken pieces, cracked the arms off the lead character, and used it to bar the door from opening easily. But it was no match for the bugbear. The improvised lock barely even slowed it down. The bugbear just smashed the glass in the door and then oozed itself through the cracks.

We backed out of the lobby as quickly as we could and into the darkened theater, tripping over Traffic Peeve, who became accidentally useful as its light-up eyes gave us glimpses of where we were going. A movie was playing on the screen. I guess someone must have started it before "the poop hit the fan", as my dad would say, but using a different word.

The movie theater was empty and kind of creepy. And not just because of what was playing on the screen. I knew *Gremlins* was one of Dad's favourites. He made us watch it a couple of years ago. It's about a furry little pet that's not supposed to eat after midnight or get wet. And of course, both of those things happen and the creature multiplies and its spawn turn into hilariously horrific monsters that overrun the town. I remembered liking it when I saw it, but I also remembered thinking how it could never happen in real life. So, obviously I was wrong about that.

As we crept down the aisle, the movie came to the scene where the gremlins are in a movie theater watching *Snow White and the Seven Dwarfs*. I think we were all caught off guard by the irony because we all paused to watch. "Life really does imitate art," said Mom. "If I were a dwarf, I'd totally be Panicky," I told Lucy, briefly remembering my very first panic attack and how that felt like a cakewalk compared to now. She smirked, then flinched when a shout rang out behind us: "Get out of there, stupid!"

We spun round, hearts pounding, to see a guy slumped down in his seat, and a peeve shouting behind him. In fact, as my eyes adjusted to the light of the projector, I noticed he was actually surrounded by peeves. They were chomping food, using phones (though I have no idea where these peeves would even get phones), and shouting gibberish at the screen.

I was about to warn him about the bugbear when it burst into the theatre and leaped onto the seats, blocking the light from the projector so that the movie looked all wobbly and dark, like it was being shown underwater. The man jumped to his feet, ready to yell at someone, only to see the bugbear looming over him, backlit by the projector. I could just make out the dark silhouettes of all the peeves it consumed earlier. The bugbear lunged, but stumbled and fell over the back row of seats, giving the man a chance to run out the way we came in. "Side effects may include drowsiness!" I shouted, excited that the pills seemed to be working.

"The exit! Hurry!" yelled Dad, pointing to the illuminated sign to the right of the screen. Traffic Peeve was already down there with its green light on for a change.

As the bugbear lumbered over the rows of theatre seats, Lucy and I finally cracked open our pill bottles. It was getting clumsier and slower with each step, but it was still trying to gobble up the uber-annoying Movie Peeves. While it ran them down, we moved towards the emergency exits. The bugbear lurched our way with a mouthful of peeves, and Lucy and I both heaved a final dose of pills just before we escaped through the exit door.

We stumbled out on to a back alley near a dumpster, which we immediately helped Mom and Dad push in front of the door. The bugbear seemed a lot weaker than it was before, but it was still plenty dangerous and there was no telling how long we had before the effect of those pills would wear off.

"What do we do?"

"Where do we go?"

"Why couldn't we just be watching *Gremlins* instead of living it?!" shouted my family members, our backs pressed against the dumpster.

All those questions made me look for Asking Peeve, but it wasn't there. None of the peeves were. That's when I noticed our remaining peeves wandering down the alley in some sort of stupor, following Sniffle Peeve, who caught a scent it really liked. You might think I'd be relieved that they were leaving, but I guess I had an instinct that they knew something we didn't. I let go of the dumpster and said, "This way!" with the sort of confidence I'm not used to having. And, much to my surprise, my family followed me.

We chased the peeves out of the alley onto a ransacked street. People and peeves were still fighting under the streetlights. Something exploded nearby, causing us to duck for cover as it lit up the night sky. That's when I saw the peeves standing one on top of the other, trying desperately to reach the handle of the door to a miraculously still-intact storefront. The sign had fallen off, but there was a light on inside. "What are you waiting for?" asked Asking Peeve in a dopey trance.

Instinctively, I scooped Asking Peeve up, pushed some rubble away, and opened the door for the rest of the peeves. As my family hurried in behind me, a little bell chimed to let the owners know they had customers. Noisy Peeve instantly made the same noise with its mouth . . . just as mine fell open.

I was face to face with Suzie Minkle.

We'd wandered into her dads' wellness centre. Suzie looked up at me from her spot on the floor, and I couldn't tell if she was happy to see me or if she was just happy to see anyone. But my peeves seemed drawn to her. Sniffle Peeve sniffed its way up to her, and not even to wipe its nose on her. Just to smell her. Crazy Peeve calmed down and sat right next to her. And to Suzie's credit, she didn't freak out. The peeves weren't trying to hurt her. They weren't even trying to annoy her. They were just . . . trying to be near her. And she actually reached out to pet them. It was the first time they looked almost cute to me.

"Are these yours?" she asked uncertainly. "I only have the one," she added, pointing to the peeve sitting in her lap. It was constantly changing shape and colour, as if it couldn't make up its mind what it wanted to be.

But before I could answer Suzie's question, Telling Peeve cut in to announce, "He like-likes you" as it snuggled Suzie's leg. My eyes went wide, my stomach dropped and I felt the old panic rise in my throat as

Suzie looked at me like I was from another planet. It was at that exact moment that her super-intimidating dads came down the back hallway. They stopped short, clearly not sure what to make of all the people and peeves – or the involuntary romantic confession directed at their daughter. I opened my mouth, but whatever I was about to say – and I have no idea what it was or if it would have even come out in coherent English – was drowned out by the loudest *roar* yet. The bugbear was still on the prowl. The medication only slowed it down, and it was getting really annoyed that it couldn't find us. Behind me I heard a click and then a crash as Lucy locked the front door and then my parents pushed over a giant display case of herbal remedies in front of it, effectively sealing us all inside my worst nightmare.

The girl I like-liked knew I like-liked her – and I'd brought a monster that wanted to eat us all to her front door.

Even now, I'm still not sure which part of that was scarier.

CHAPTER 11

THE SIDE EFFECTS

There are few things in life more terrifying than letting someone know exactly how you feel. At the top of that list would be doing so while a monstrous bugbear is hunting you down.

And that's what was happening to me as I stood inside Minkle Meditations, the yoga and wellness centre run by Suzie's dads, Chad and Brad Minkle. They weren't thrilled that Mom and Dad had knocked over their display case, but they joined my parents at the blinds to try to catch a glimpse of what was causing all the chaos. Mom and Dad were keeping an eye out for the bugbear, but those pills seemed to have bought us some time. That's when the Minkles noticed my frozen state.

"Don't be embarrassed," said Brad, an Asian guy who had the wiry frame of a rock star with a buzz cut and tattoo sleeves made up of natural elements and Buddhist symbols. My cheeks felt hot enough to fry an egg on, but something about the Electric Mayhem Muppets T-shirt Brad was wearing made him seem a little less intimidating. "You can be your authentic self here," he continued in a commanding tone that suggested it wasn't a suggestion at all.

"That being said, we can be our authentic selves as well," added Chad, a white dude with the thicker build of an action movie star who did not have a cartoon T-shirt to offset my fear. "Which means you better be careful what you say next," he added as a broad smirk split his reddish beard. He and Brad both crossed their arms in sync like two superheroes after they'd defeated the bad guy.

"Dads! Ugh. Stop," was all Suzie could say as she stood up and turned away from them, embarrassed. That made me feel a little better. At least I wasn't the only one feeling uncomfortable. Her dads instantly dropped the tough guy act.

"Do you guys have any idea what these things are?" asked Chad, motioning to the peeves.

"We've been trying to lay low and avoid the agitation outside, but we'd love some answers," added Brad.

"It's a long story," said Dad as he and Mom finally stepped away from the window to introduce themselves.

Asking Peeve looked up at me, staring at the ground,

practically holding my breath. It wanted to know, "Why are you holding it in?" And it was right.

I exhaled and looked up at Suzie. "These are my peeves. They started when I got sprayed in the face with an experimental anti-anxiety treatment called Personal Vexation Zoners, or PVZ, at Clarity Labs. I wanted to tell you about it in the supply closet, but I didn't know at the time what was going on. I just thought I'd got crazier. I didn't know it was contagious or that it would evolve into a big bugbear, which eats peeves and is chasing us now. And that's just *my* bugbear. No one else seems to have hit stage two yet. But I think they will. And there's probably another stage coming after that. Maybe more. I don't see how it could be worse, but supposedly it will be. And you smell really nice, and I know that we don't really have time for that right now but you do. The whole world might be ending, and your dads are kind of scaring me, and we have to find a way to stop it all before it's too late!"

Everyone stared at me wide-eyed as I went back to holding my breath. Chad and Brad nodded and tried to pretend like they understood any of what I'd said. The only thing all the parents really latched onto was the least important part.

"What closet?" asked Dad.

"Why were you in there?" demanded Chad.

"And what were you doing?" added Brad, crossing his tattooed arms again.

"We are going to talk about this later!" concluded Mom.

But Suzie broke through the parental hostility to tell me, "Wow . . . You should probably breathe now."

Chad and Brad instinctively breathed deeply – just like one of the yoga or meditation classes they taught. And my whole family involuntarily followed along.

"Breathe in for five, and out for five," they guided. It actually felt really calming, like maybe I hadn't ever breathed correctly before. The Minkles were the total opposite of my family. Where we were all scattered and closed off, they were all calm and open. At least, that's what it seemed for the first few breaths. Then Suzie snapped.

"They're not customers! Can we stop pretending to be perfect for a minute? We all have peeves! Even you!" she said as she pointed at the two peeves that stepped out from behind her dads.

Chad's peeve was bigger, cleaner and firmer than the other peeves. It literally looked down on all of them. It had its arms crossed and a half smile on its face, like it was thinking of a joke that no one else would get. It gave the lot of us a disappointed once-over. "She's right. You're being dense," it said up at Chad. "And your core is not as tight as it should be. An eight pack is the new six pack." I'd say this was Judging Peeve, and I was really happy I didn't have one of those to deal with.

Brad's peeve was more hesitant. It was frail and hunched-over and looked nervous, like it didn't know quite what to do with its paws, like it was trying to be cooler than it was. "Maybe if you try harder. Or try less. Or maybe if you just don't do anything. Maybe then nobody will notice that you don't know what to do." Doubting Peeve. Definitely Doubting Peeve. Which made me feel better. Is that wrong to say? But the fact that a couple of guys who looked this cool on the outside had their own issues on the inside made me feel a little less insecure.

"Sweetie, we're just trying to rise above," said Chad.

"Acknowledge your feelings and let them go," reminded Brad.

"I am acknowledging my feelings! It's right here, staring at me!" replied Suzie, pointing at her very own peeve. It was changing shape and colour and attitude so quickly I felt a little nauseous watching it. "I'm tired of trying to be calm and centred all the time! It makes me feel like I don't know who I really am." And that's when her Wannabe Peeve matched the colour of Suzie's clothes and added, "I just want to fit in."

I guess constant, total Zen can be hard to maintain, especially when it's being foisted upon you by your parents. Suzie shoved Wannabe Peeve away from her and walked across the room . . . with every single peeve following her. She stopped short, a little freaked out. "Why are they doing that?!" she said as she moved in another direction and the peeves did too. "Why are they following me?" she said as she backed into the toppled display case, causing the door to open and vials of essential oils to roll out on the floor.

"You're like the Pied Piper of peeves," said Lucy as Sniffle Peeve sniffed its way through the vials, picking up a particular one and sniffing it super hard. Suzie grabbed it away and read the label: "Eucalyptus oil."

"That's what we use during massages," said Brad. "It helps calm the nervous system . . . but . . . what was that about an even bigger monster chasing you guys?"

"Is that . . . still out there?" added Chad, trying to keep calm, but, based on the shakiness of his voice, not quite succeeding.

Mom and Dad started to fill them in as Suzie opened

the vial and squeezed a drop of eucalyptus oil onto her finger. Then she took my hand and rubbed it on my wrist. I could feel my face flush bright red. "It's what I dab on myself every day to remember to chill out," she said, "even though I still need to hide in the closet and read creepy comics sometimes."

And speaking of centred, I was suddenly the centre of a lot of attention. Fifteen little monsters, including the Minkles' Judging and Doubting and Wannabe Peeves, followed the smell right over to me, lining up like they did to Suzie. Every move I made, they followed.

"It's like catnip!" concluded Lucy, who looked relieved that Copy Peeve was too focused on the smell to bother repeating her for once.

"So THAT'S why they got so calm when we were in the closet today!" I said before getting the fatherly glares from Brad and Chad that made me realise I should probably avoid ever mentioning being in the closet with Suzie again. At the time, I thought Suzie had calmed the peeves herself, but apparently the peeves were all about this funky aromatherapy stuff. The only thing Suzie actually calmed in that closet was me.

I was so embarrassed, but then I caught Suzie

looking at me like she never had before. "You must have been totally freaking out in there," she said as she pieced the events of the day together. "But I gotta say, right now you seem better adjusted than any of us." That was a first. But when I looked around I saw two sets of panicking parents worried about the bugbear on the loose, a sister who was vacillating wildly from self-sufficient to self-doubting, and the calmest, coolest girl I knew revealing that she's struggling to figure herself out just as much as the rest of us. "It's nice," Suzie continued, "I mean, personal growth is cool, right?"

In all my attempts to deal with my anxiety issues, I had suffered plenty of unpleasant side effects, but I had never experienced a pleasant one until that exact moment. Somehow, in the middle of this nightmare, and with unasked-for assistance from Telling Peeve, I made an honest connection with someone I liked. Go figure.

"Guys . . ." Lucy cut in. But Mom and Dad and Brad and Chad were listening in that way grown-ups do when they somehow hear what kids are saying and completely ignore them at the same time.

"Should we call for help?" asked Mom.

"The landlines are down and mobile coverage is spotty," said Chad.

"They must have taken out the closest tower," added Brad.

The eucalyptus oil had already worn off because Worry Peeve started to worry again and the duelling Bossy Peeves began arguing about which one of them had the best plan to save us all – "We should run." "We should hide." "We should fight." "We should surrender."

I looked at Suzie and she shrugged. "Did you really think a nice smell would be a permanent fix?"

"Guys!" said Lucy again. And this time, Copy Peeve dopily broke away from the peeves lined up by me and echoed her at the top of its voice. To no avail.

"What about a car?" suggested Dad. "We could try to get to the hospital again."

"It's too far," said Chad. "The TV news said the roads are blocked."

Lucy grabbed Noisy Peeve and squeezed it really hard, forcing out one long *BEEEEEEEEEEEEEEP!*

Everyone finally turned to her. She dropped Noisy Peeve, instantly realising that might have been a mistake. She told us in a whisper, "The bugbear is coming!"

The streetlight outside cast a growing shadow of the bugbear on the blinds as it approached the wellness centre. None of us moved. We barely even breathed.

The shadow paused at the door, but then moved past. And that's when I noticed Noisy Peeve trembling. I silently warned it not to. We locked eyes. It nodded like it understood, but it couldn't hold it in for long. Its mouth opened. I made a break for it, hoping I could stifle the sound, but I was too late. Noisy Peeve went off like a geyser:

BEEP BEEP BEEP
CRASH
FART
WHOOSH
WEE-OOO WEE-OO
DING-DONG, DING-DONG!

And then Noisy Peeve relaxed, emptied like a deflated balloon, while the rest of us braced for the consequences. For a few moments, nothing happened. I didn't dare say it, but I thought that maybe the bugbear somehow hadn't heard. I let out a sigh and started to relax.

And then: SMASH!

The bugbear crashed through the window, gobbling up Noisy Peeve before it could even get the satisfaction of mimicking the sound of the breaking glass. The last we heard from it was a sad, muffled *BLURP BOOP BLOP* sound like the dying police siren the bugbear had squashed earlier. The other peeves scattered and the rest of us followed Brad and Chad past the yoga and acupuncture and massage rooms as the bugbear squeezed down the narrow hallway behind us.

"Is Slim gonna get eaten? Is he gonna be okay? We have to save him," came the worries of Worry Peeve one last time as it jumped off Lucy's shoulder to make sure I had got to safety. But I was already up ahead and actually felt kind of bad I couldn't stop the bugbear from swallowing Worry Peeve in one big, sloppy gulp.

"You should chew before you swallow," instructed Mom's Bossy Peeve.

"And cover your mouth if you burp," added Lucy's Bossy Peeve.

The bugbear gobbled them both up, swallowed them whole, and let out a juicy *BURRRRRP* just to spite them.

With each peeve it ate, the bugbear grew a little bigger and a lot angrier. But the bigger it got, the harder it became for the monster to fit down the hall. "Here! Into the storage room," urged Brad, guiding us all in first before slamming and locking the door behind us. But the bugbear wasn't giving up that easily. It threw itself against the door again and again until the doorframe started to splinter and break.

"The back door, quick!" said Chad, fumbling with the multiple locks as the bugbear smashed the storage-room door off its frame. The only thing keeping it out was that the door fell against a tall shelf, allowing only a tight, angular opening for the bugbear to ooze through. And it was having trouble this time. It unleashed its gross, gummy tongue, slapping around inside, trying to grab us. As Lucy ducked, its tongue hit a shelf of acupuncture needles, spilling them onto the floor. Suzie grabbed a handful of needles and started throwing them at the monster, and we all followed her lead. Enough of them stuck in painful spots on the tongue to make the bugbear pull back and *ROAR*.

"That's not proper acupuncture technique," criticised Judging Peeve. "You'll never succeed." It turned to lecture us right before the bugbear's needle-covered tongue swung back in, snatched the peeve round its neck and retracted into its mouth like it was slurping up a long, wet noodle.

The bugbear pushed against the doorframe with all its strength, causing it to warp and break under its weight, creating just enough room for it to squeeze halfway in. Crazy Peeve freaked out and started grabbing anything it could get its paws on – every random supplement bottle, every box of cotton swabs

182

– and just tossing them at the bugbear as fast as it could (which was way faster than any of us could manage). Before I could even start to wonder what the needles and all those pills would do to the monster, I heard the exit door click open.

"Let's go!" Chad yelled as the bugbear finally broke the door down. But Suzie let go of her dads and ran right back in.

"Suzie!" yelled Brad. Wannabe Peeve had gone with her, desperate to be part of the action. The bugbear lunged for Suzie, but Wannabe Peeve jumped in front of her, trying to be heroic like it thought Suzie was doing, and was gobbled whole for it instead. Suzie ducked and rolled and grabbed something in one fluid yoga-inspired motion. She then slid under the bugbear and ran back outside, right past her dads with a whole box of eucalyptus oil. "Just in case!" she said as Brad slammed the door shut on the bugbear with a *CLICK* of the lock.

I backed away from the door, catching my breath with the others.

"He peed himself," said Telling Peeve, pointing at me.

"No, I didn't!" I yelled defensively. "You're not even in my head any more. How would you know?"

Telling Peeve pointed a little lower at a tiny wet spot on my crotch. "Just a little," it said as I instantly covered it, humiliated.

Luckily, no one was paying attention to us. They were all too distracted by the fact that there were now a dozen globs of black goo in various stages of bugbear formation all over town.

"I thought there was only one bugbear!" shouted Suzie.

"There was." I gulped.

"This must be stage three," said Lucy.

"I don't think so," I replied as multiple new bugbears *ROARED* to life.

My heart sank as I realised what was happening: "This is just everyone else catching up to stage two."

CHAPTER 12

THE HOMECOMING

All the new bugbears formed the same way mine had in the car: fast and furious.

The black goo all around us doubled, tripled and quadrupled in size so fast their previous human hosts could only stand and stare, not realising that as soon as the bugbears sprouted legs, they would be after them, eating every peeve they could get their gooey mouths on, and any person that got in their way.

"If they have bugbears, where's mine?! I was exposed next!" shouted Lucy.

"I guess results really do vary," I responded, not necessarily calming her down.

"We have to get away from here," said Dad just before hearing the *BLEEP-BLOOP KA-CHUNK* of a car being unlocked remotely. I spun round to see Chad and Brad rush to their Prius and open the doors.

"C'mon," Chad said, calling us all over. "Hurry!"

"We're never going to fit in there!" Mom yelled as

my bugbear started to break through a security window in the storage room. "We'll squeeze!" she decided as she herded the rest of us into the compact car anyway. Minkles up front, Pickings in the back. Asking, Telling, Crazy, Sniffle, Copy, Ignoring, Deadline and Doubting Peeves squished wherever they could fit in between.

"You kind of like us," said Telling Peeve as Sniffle Peeve wiped its nose on my trousers, then looked at me kind of apologetically like it couldn't help it.

"Well, you're better than a bugbear," was my reply.

Chad threw the car in gear and peeled out of the parking lot, but we didn't even make it onto Main Street before he hit the brakes. Right in front of us was Dad's Traffic Peeve "directing" the chaos like a cop, but really it was just randomly signalling like it was having a seizure. People and peeves filled the street but they all ignored Traffic Peeve's frantic orders and flashing eyes. It was just one more annoying peeve among thousands.

"Just run it over!" yelled Dad. But it wasn't Traffic Peeve that Chad was avoiding. One of the newly formed bugbears charged from across the street, heading right for us. Traffic Peeve seemed unfazed, simply trying to help the bugbear cross the road, which is exactly where it went – with its mouth open. And that was the last we saw of Traffic Peeve. The bugbear *ROARED* at us just as my bugbear oozed its way out of the security window, taking the wall down with it.

Chad threw the car into reverse and floored it, speeding backwards through the parking lot and into an alleyway. "Get down! I can't see!" he shouted. But there was no room to breathe, much less to move with seven people and eight peeves in a Prius built for five. Chad rolled down the driver's side window and stuck his head out. "Don't worry. I used to be a licensed stunt driver," he reassured us.

"That's how we met," said Brad. "I gave him acupuncture to help with the pain after he crashed and almost died." Which normally must have been a totally romantic story, but right then it just made a scary moment downright terrifying.

We peeled round a corner and I thought we were in the clear when another bugbear came out of nowhere and sideswiped us as it gobbled up more peeves. The car spun three times, skidding around until we were back facing the right way. "Oh, that's better," said Chad as he threw the car into drive and sped away. He was weaving through the mayhem and obstacles like, well, a licensed stunt driver. We were getting away until two more bugbears leaped into our path.

Chad tried to get round them, but the car pinballed off one and then the other. We spun left and then right. I thought I was going to throw up, which Telling Peeve noticed. "He's gonna puke!" it shouted. But there was nowhere to move. If I was going to hurl, we were all going to get hit with it. So I swallowed down my nausea, and Chad cut a sidewalk corner, knocking over a garbage can filled, to my surprise, with filthy Garbage Peeves before hauling off down a side street.

"This car wasn't built to take such a beating, I'm not sure it'll last much longer," said Chad as he cut through a bunch of traffic cones to find a clearer path on the newly paved section of road we passed earlier. He had to slam through the flattened, burned-out portaloo, causing its contents to SPLATTER on the windshield, leaving the orange, sewage-covered face of that Hateful Peeve I saw get run over by the steamroller earlier squashed like a bug on the glass in front of Chad, blocking his view.

"Your lifestyle is disgusting!" yelled Hateful Peeve at the Minkles as it tried to reinflate itself.

"Says the monster covered in poop"! yelled Chad, who definitely didn't say "poop". He flipped on the windshield wipers, smearing Hateful Peeve back and forth across the glass while trying to get a clear view of where we were going.

"Maybe you shouldn't have married such an aggressive guy," said Doubting Peeve to Brad, who looked stunned.

Chad shot him a surprised look. "I love you!" was Brad's reaffirming response as the car jerked and swerved again. The engine was starting to rattle and smoke.

Crazy Peeve smushed my face against the window, pointing excitedly and jabbering, "Inky purple jabba jabba!" Before I knew it, the whole car shook with a CRUNCH as a bugbear landed on top and wrapped its dark purple legs round the sides of the car.

"It's crushing us!" shouted Suzie as the roof collapsed a bit.

"Fake news!" shouted Hateful Peeve just before the bugbear crushed it into the cracking windshield and slurped it up and out of sight for good.

"We have to get somewhere safe!" I yelled.

"We can't go anywhere with this thing on us!" Lucy screamed.

"It's breaking the windows!" my parents shrieked in unison.

But Chad hit the gas, picking up speed so fast all the peeves inside were splatted against the rear window.

We were heading straight for a one-lane, low-clearance tunnel.

"Chad, I know you're used to surviving stunts," said Brad as he braced himself, "but the rest of us are not!"

SPLAT! SMASH! KA-CLUNK!

Chad drove the bugbear straight into the concrete arch above us, knocking it off the roof as we sped through the tunnel. It smashed through the windows in an effort to hold on, but the force of impact sent the monster bouncing off down the road behind us. I spun round and peeled Asking Peeve off the rear window so I could make sure the bugbear was gone.

The car was now wobbling and the smoke spewing from the engine was so thick it was hard to see through it. "This car is on its last legs," warned Chad as he took another turn. "And AAA is not gonna help us out here. We need to take cover!"

"Can we just go home?" cried Lucy.

"Which home?" I replied.

"The model home!" screamed Mom, grabbing at Chad and pointing left.

Chad swerved as another bugbear cut us off. The Prius skidded to a stop, reversed and then spun its tyres as Brad reached over and pulled the wheel and yelled, "Our home is that way!"

But another bugbear was already trashing that street. Chad yanked the wheel back with an aggressively Zen, "Sweetie, I don't touch your needles, so you don't touch my wheel. Don't make me get authentic on you!"

"Just keep your chi in check . . . and also keep the car on four wheels!" Brad said, letting go as I redoubled my focus on not getting carsick.

My face was pressed against the window, next to Asking Peeve, who had just finished reinflating in time to wonder, "What's a home?"

"It's where a family lives," I replied as I spotted a clear road that had somehow avoided being destroyed so far. And it was a road I knew very well. "Or where our family *used* to live. Turn right!" I shouted, "I know where to go!"

Chad spun the wheel, dashing narrowly round the legs of a bugbear that was charging the other way, gobbling up some of the only remaining peeves on the street. We headed up a hilly road that hadn't yet been ransacked and I pointed out the next turn.

"Good call," said Lucy when she realised where we were going. I turned round and peered out of the back window. The town was trashed behind us – smoke billowing and sirens wailing in the night sky. And although we got a head start, it wouldn't be long till the bugbears caught up.

Chad parked the car in our old driveway about two seconds before it sputtered out and died. Everyone hopped out of the smoking vehicle except for Mom and Dad, who let me and Lucy and the peeves climb out over them as they just stared at the two-storey Craftsman house for an uncomfortable beat. It had been a long time since they "came home" together. "It looks . . . different," I heard Dad say.

"The new owners wanted it fumigated before they moved in," was all Mom could muster in response.

"Probably a good idea. Pests are bad," replied Dad before they finally stepped out on opposite sides, not really wanting to look at each other.

"Is this a home? Is this YOUR home? Is this OUR home?" asked Asking Peeve.

"It used to be, but it's not any more," I answered honestly.

"I liked it better blue," said Lucy.

"It feels like bizarro world," I agreed.

It had been months since I'd been here. And seeing it now was like a dream. Things were familiar, but off. It was weird. The house was beige where it used to be blue, and there were different flowers out front and a new and functioning porch swing to replace the one I broke and blamed on Lucy. But the weirdest part was probably the sign out front screaming that it's been "SOLD!" That meant some new family would be moving in any day now. Some new kid would be sleeping in my room and climbing the crabapple tree out back. "Bizarro world" was an understatement. And it wasn't just because there was a circuslike fumigation tent half pinned to one side of the house and half on the lawn, or an abandoned Buzz-Off Pest Control van at the bottom of the driveway. It was because *we* weren't the same. And standing in front of our old home with my whole family, I realised that even though we were technically the same people, we'd undergone a renovation just as much as our old house had. But it wasn't finished yet.

Lucy found the key under the welcome mat and took the Minkles inside.

"Can I go inside? Can I see a home? Can I see bizarro world?" came the questions from Asking Peeve. I nodded yes, and it bounded through the door before my parents, who were distracted by Deadline Peeve informing us all that "Stage three is coming. Any minute. It's almost too late!" Mom and Dad took that in with a synchronised gulp and hurried inside.

The other peeves followed behind, all except Ignoring Peeve, who pretended not to notice where we were going. Dad went to close the door, but I held it for a second and yelled to Ignoring Peeve to come inside. But it just did what Ignoring Peeves do and ignored me as it blended into the grass. "Those peeves aren't our problem, Slim," Dad said before catching himself. "I mean, that's exactly what they are, but we need to look out for each other, not them."

I knew Dad was right and stepped back to let the door close, but Deadline Peeve pushed past and put its foot in the jamb. It held the door open just wide enough to shout out at Ignoring Peeve, "Get in here! Time is running out!" But Ignoring Peeve simply turned its back. Sniffle Peeve ducked under Deadline Peeve's arm and went outside to try to get Ignoring Peeve inside. But Ignoring Peeve just walked away like it hadn't heard or seen a thing, blending into the paved driveway even though Sniffle Peeve was only two steps behind it and sniffling loudly enough to hear from all the way on the front porch. Crazy Peeve couldn't take it any more and bounded outside like one of those numbered Ping-Pong balls they use for lottery drawings, trying to get Ignoring Peeve's attention, but Ignoring Peeve ignored it too. Telling

Peeve stepped out in front of me, pointed my way, and said, "He wants us to go inside!" Copy Peeve picked up on that and ran outside shouting, "Go inside! Go inside!" But then Doubting Peeve second-guessed that idea. "Or maybe we should all go *outside*," it said as Mom, Lucy and the Minkles joined us at the door to see it do just that.

"Are they . . . helping it?" asked Mom, totally surprised.

"Self-preservation is a natural instinct," said Chad.

"They care about each other," said Suzie.

"It's almost . . . human," I concluded.

But the moment ended when Ignoring Peeve finally saw something it couldn't pretend wasn't there – a bugbear. It *ROARED* as it burst through the tall bushes separating properties, and despite Ignoring Peeve's best camouflage, the bugbear gobbled it up without even slowing down.

Dad slammed the door, locked the deadbolt and then pushed a fancy credenza in front as a barricade.

"That's an antique!" Mom yelled instinctively.

"And it would be nice if we had the chance to become one too!" Dad snapped back.

"Good point." Mom shrugged, grabbing another piece of unpronounceable furniture and hefting it on top. We all pitched in, barricading the doors and windows with whatever we could find as the bugbear chased the peeves around the Prius outside. Finally, the bugbear lost its patience and smashed the car flat. From the window, I saw Copy Peeve imitate that foot-stomping movement and I could just barely hear Doubting Peeve yelling, "That may have been a bad idea," as they were both swallowed whole. Crazy Peeve went nuts in the bugbear's face and got swatted away, splatting on the window I was looking through.

"There's another stage coming to replace you soon," I could hear Deadline Peeve shouting at the bugbear outside. "Your time is almost up!" it warned the monster. But it was apparently Deadline Peeve whose time was up, since the bugbear ate it without a second thought.

Asking Peeve popped up next to me, seemingly the only peeve left. It peeked through the curtain, looking for its lost peeve buddies. "Why do bad things happen to good peeves?" it asked.

I didn't know how to answer that, but Dad pulled the curtain shut and shoved a bookshelf in front of the window, saying, "As far as I'm concerned, good things just happened to bad peeves."

Asking Peeve looked hurt by that and I was actually about to say something in its defence when I heard the bugbear destroy something else in the front yard before moving round towards the back of the house. "We're safe in here, right?" asked Suzie.

Dad glanced around, making sure all the ways in or out were secured when I guess he also noticed all the changes to the house. It was still the same open space with a super-high vaulted ceiling and stairs leading to the upstairs hallway that overlooked the room below, but even with half the furniture piled up against the door and windows, he could see that it now had a sleeker, far more modern design than the frumpy, comfy furnishings we used to lounge on. He frowned. "I hate what you've done with the place."

Mom's face dropped. "Luckily the new owners have better taste than you."

Before they could start to fight, the moment was blown apart by Lucy's massive sneeze. A giant glob of black goo splatted on the floor by the front door and immediately started to stretch and grow. "Oh no, you hit stage two!" shouted Mom just before she sneezed as well. Her black goo splatted by the living-room window. I backed away. I knew what was coming. But I bumped into Chad and Brad staring gape-mouthed in the middle of the room.

"That's it, right?" said Suzie. "It's not like we're all

gonna . . ." And then she sneezed too, shooting black goo all over the kitchen floor. Brad and Chad stepped in front of her protectively, but then Brad sneezed on Chad and Chad sneezed on Brad. They quickly wiped it off themselves, flinging it across the room.

"This isn't good . . . This really isn't goo . . . goo . . . ACHOOOO!" came the final sneeze from Dad.

And as his black goo landed at the bottom of the stairs, we found ourselves surrounded by blobs of growing bugbears. "This might not be good, but it's definitely goo," confirmed Lucy in a trembling voice.

"Why didn't you see that coming?" asked Asking Peeve, hiding behind my leg. And I didn't have a good answer. I just got so caught up in running away from the bugbears the people in town had already released that I forgot about the inevitable bugbears my friends and family would create. But there was no time to be self-critical. Six big, bad, blobs were rising up all around us. Even if we hadn't boarded up all the exits, there would have been no way out. We had trapped ourselves in a house that wasn't even our home any more.

"There's only one peeve left," said Suzie as we clustered together in the middle of the room. "And these bugbears already look hungry," she added while sidestepping one of the gooey, chomping mouths developing all around us.

And then Asking Peeve asked the question I think we were all wondering:

"What will they eat next?"

CHAPTER 13

THE LEVEL-UP

"Upstairs! Run!" I yelled. And surprisingly, once again, everyone actually listened to me. Not that there was much choice. There were six hungry new bugbears in various stages of formation cutting off every exit out of the house on the ground floor. Lucy led the way up, and I picked up the tail, leaping over the most recent and least developed bugbear at the foot of the stairs. It was only a mouth with no eyes or legs yet, so we were all able to jump over it one by one – except Asking Peeve. It got snagged in midair by the bugbear's newly developed tongue. I grabbed Asking Peeve's arm and yanked it free a half second before the bugbear swallowed it. That really annoyed it as two angry red eyes popped up in its head, glaring at me in a rage.

The other bugbears *ROARED* and came after us as best they could on their still-forming legs. One of them lunged for me and just missed, smashing and splintering the stair railing. The other bugbears piled on, scrambling over each other to get up the stairs. The stairs creaked and cracked under their weight. Then . . . *KER-CRUNCH* – the entire staircase broke away and collapsed just as I hit the landing. I wobbled backwards and almost fell, but Mom and Dad grabbed me just in time.

We were all safely stranded in the upstairs hallway, while the bugbears had actually fallen right through the ground floor and into a pile of broken stairs in the basement. I peered over the edge of the upstairs hallway. All six angry bugbears were stuck in the dark, unfinished concrete cellar, desperate to figure out how to reach us.

"Good thing I insisted on high ceilings," said Mom. And she was right. Her design sense put a lot more distance between us and the seven-foot-tall bugbears than your average house would have. But even so, I knew it would only be a matter of time before they would figure out a way to reach us, or knock the whole house down trying.

And right on cue, one of the bugbears leaped up and got its pawlike forelegs on the carpet edge of the living room below. Fortunately, the thread unravelled from its weight and the bugbear fell, legs reeling, and landed with a splat. A glass and steel decorative end table fell down after it, shattering on its head. It lay still, shocked from the impact. But then the other bugbears stepped on top of it, using the first bugbear's end-table-encased head as a stepladder to get back to the ground floor.

"They're making a bugbear ladder!" shouted Suzie.

"Dale, the attic!" cried Mom. Dad ran down the hall and pulled down the door, unfolding a stepladder from above. The bugbears already seemed to be on us. They were leaping at us and lashing their tongues all around on the landing. They knocked over paint cans and spilled everything out of a toolbox Mom had left behind.

Weapons! we all seemed to realise at once as we snatched up the hammers and wrenches and screwdrivers and spun round to battle back the bugbears. Even Asking Peeve joined in, rolling a full can of paint down the hall and onto the head of a monster below. But Mom went hardcore. Wielding a nail gun, she fired down at the bugbears, nailing them to the floor. I think it was more satisfying than effective – the monsters just kept pulling their gummy bodies free – but man, was it satisfying to watch.

I could see four of the bugbears in the living room. Two were climbing all over each other, trying to get to us, and two were lashing out at the walls and doing some serious structural damage to the house. The other two were still stuck in the basement. The one thing I knew for sure was that we wouldn't be able to keep them at bay much longer. Mom must have realised the same thing because she suddenly yelled, "Everyone to the attic – now!"

The Minkles went up first, and then Dad started helping Lucy. But something fell out of her pocket and she stopped to pick it up. It was the last pill bottle from the pharmacy.

"No more refills," she said as she tossed it to me and scrambled up the ladder.

I hurried over to the edge just as Mom ran out of nails. The four bugbears in the living room were temporarily pinned to the floor and not happy about it. They *ROARED* up at us, and so I took the opportunity and tossed the pills down into their gaping mouths like it was some sort of awful arcade game. I threw the empty bottle at one of them for good measure.

"The monsters need them more than you do right now," said Mom. And I kind of smiled at the truth of it.

Dad came over to hurry us up into the attic. He took a second to check out the bugbears and he seemed relieved that they were already becoming sluggish and clumsy. They seemed to have less energy to prise themselves free – and when one of them did, it just sort of fell over. But even so, they wouldn't give up. They were just attacking us much more slowly. "They're relentless," Dad said.

"Who lives in there?" asked Asking Peeve, peering from behind my leg to point to my room behind us. Or what used to be my room. It was redecorated in red, white and blue faux-Americana like a page from a Fourth of July-themed Pottery Barn catalogue.

"Me," I answered, "or it used to be me. Now it must be Captain America Junior."

I cast an accusing look at Mom and she instantly cringed and said, "I know, I know. It was a special request."

Dad was getting really impatient. "I know it's not on any of your schedules, but could you please come up to the attic now?" he asked Mom. "It would be great if we got away before those things shake off their medication and see where we're hiding."

One of the bugbears collapsed. Then another fell on top of it. Then another. And suddenly the least dosed of the pack started climbing up their bodies, giving it just enough height to reach the landing.

Asking Peeve leaped back and climbed up onto my shoulder to get away, and we all hurried for the attic.

Dad made sure Mom was up first, and then he reached for me as the bugbear tripped over its own legs and face-planted at my feet. I had just stepped onto the ladder when I felt something cold and sticky and gross wrap round my ankle, yanking me down. The bugbear got me with its tongue like a frog snaring a bug!

Asking Peeve fell off my shoulder as I slid down the ladder and across the hallway, getting a painful rug burn. My foot was just about in the bugbear's mouth when Asking Peeve ran up and sank its own teeth into the bugbear's tongue, causing it to release its grip on me. "It doesn't feel good, does it?" taunted Asking Peeve as Dad grabbed my hand, hoisting both of us up into the attic. The bugbear had just got back on its feet as Dad pulled the stairs up and slammed the door shut in its face.

He tied the rope off to a beam so it couldn't be pulled open from below. Then he looked at me. And I looked at everyone else. And we all looked around us.

We were trapped. There was no escape.

CHAPTER 14

THE EXTRACTION

It must have been a hundred degrees in the attic. Dust swirled in the dim light from the lone bulb in the ceiling. The roof angled in at us and only a tiny bit of moonlight came through the small window in the dormer at the front. The air smelled musty and old and made it all feel smaller and tighter than it actually was. In any other circumstances, on any other day, being trapped up there would have totally thrown me into a claustrophobic panic. But at that moment I had bigger things to worry about than my own discomfort.

"Did the pills work?" asked Suzie. She was standing awkwardly between her dads, who had to stoop to stand up in our attic. "Did they slow them down?"

"A bit – but that won't last long," I told her. I had enough experience with these medications, and the bugbears, to know this wouldn't be the whole solution. "We're treating the symptoms, not the cause," I explained. "We need to find a more permanent solution if we're going to stop them."

"Mobile coverage is working here. You guys have to see this," said Lucy, who was hunched over her phone watching a live streaming news report.

We all gathered round the screen and saw that the roads had been blocked off and forensic scientists in full biohazard gear were setting up shop.

"Reports of chemical-induced hysteria are coming out of the coastal town of Old Wayford, Connecticut, today," the reporter said as the camera cut to distant shots of peeve and bugbear-incited chaos, even though the reporter clearly couldn't see what was really happening. "The residents seem to be in the throes of a mass hallucination. The Centre for Disease Control is quarantining the town until it can deduce the origins of the outbreak and how contagious it might be."

I looked up at everyone else. "The CDC people, whoever they are . . . How can they help if they can't even see what they're supposed to be stopping?" I asked, even though I already knew the answer. There wouldn't be any help coming.

Everyone started searching the attic for any possible thing that could help us survive. But really, all we managed to find were a couple of forgotten boxes of useless knick-knacks and memories. "I can't believe I missed these," said Mom. There were Lucy's Junior soccer trophies and the watercolour landscapes Mom painted that summer she took a class, and even Dad's old CD collection, which I thought he'd thrown away after I helped him rip them all onto his computer years ago.

"What's this?" asked Asking Peeve, holding up an old digital photo frame, accidentally clicking a button and lighting the room a bit more with some of the good times we once had. Mom, Dad and Lucy came over to my corner to look. There was a photo of me covered in pizza sauce at my sixth birthday at Chuck E. Cheese. That dissolved into one of Lucy climbing the crabapple tree, then the day Mom and Dad moved into this house, and then one of me water-skiing on Big Moose Lake. I remembered that right after Mom took that picture I hit a wave and face-planted into the water.

"Wow. We almost look happy," said Lucy, and Mom and Dad shared that look grown-ups get when they're caught doing something wrong but don't want to acknowledge it.

"Yeah, it's easy to look that way from the outside," Suzie said, throwing her dads some serious side-eye.

"Now is not a good time to be passive-aggressive, Suzie," warned Chad as he pointed at the attic door being rattled by the bugbear trying to get in from below. Clearly, the medication had worn off.

"Remember your calming affirmations," added Brad, as if by rote. "Be the change you want to see in the world," he concluded in an utterly unconvincing daze.

And then Suzie snapped.

"Stop telling me what to be! I can't be calm and Zen and let my bothersome thoughts float out of my head all the time – and neither can you! Do you know how much it bothers me to overlook everything that bothers me?!"

But before anyone could muster an answer the door bounced with a thump from the angry bugbear below. Chad tried to hold it closed as Suzie continued. "You're not the perfect Zen masters you want everyone to think you are. No one is. That's why we're trapped up here! It's not possible to never have bad feelings! I feel bad all the time!"

"Join the club," said Lucy. "At least your parents don't ignore you."

Mom took that personally. "We do not do that," she insisted unconvincingly. She looked to Dad before asking, "Do we?"

Dad shrugged. "We haven't been great about sticking to our schedules," he admitted. "And she was right about the PVZ and I didn't listen." Mom couldn't argue with that. The bugbear rattled the door again, hard enough this time that the rope came loose.

Mom and Dad ran over to tie it off again as Brad and Chad held it shut. But Suzie wasn't done expressing herself just yet. "Sometimes I actually want to be annoyed and angry. Sometimes I don't want to let it go!"

The bugbear slammed into the attic door, and our parents strained to hold it shut.

"None of this would even be happening if you just listened to us in the first place!" cried Lucy. "The divorce made things so much worse." Our parents were bouncing up and down as the hinges on the door broke loose and it fell down below, swinging right into the face of the bugbear, knocking it back and nearly taking them with it.

"Your father and I are not getting back together," Mom shot back as they rushed away from the exposed door. A tongue lashed up, smashing out the lone light bulb, plunging us into darkness, but for the dim moonlight through the little window.

"No one is asking you to!" I snapped, surprising

everyone. "We don't need you back together. We need you to get your poop together!" Except I didn't say "poop".

For a moment, Mom and Dad wore exactly the same shocked expression, but then we heard a huge crash below.

Brad took a quick peek out of the attic, then dived back as a bugbear tongue tried to get him. "Yeah, they knocked half the landing down and now there are four not-so-drugged-up bugbears climbing the wreckage to the hallway under us," he said as we all scattered.

"Can we climb out of here?" asked Lucy, running over to the window at the far end of the attic. I raced after her and looked outside. But the window was a decorative part of the dormer and wasn't meant to open. Our house was up on a hill and we had a pretty good view of the town. Between the streetlamps and moonlight, even in the dark we could see there were bugbears everywhere. I watched two bugbears toss the Minkles' flattened Prius at a couple of peeves they were chasing across our front yard. The wrecked car blocked their escape and the bugbears swallowed them whole. Asking Peeve stood next to me, looking sad and confused about what it saw. It held the digital photo frame to its chest and asked, "Where is my home?" At first, I wasn't sure what to tell it, but then I looked out of the window and pointed off into the distance to the faint, moonlit sight of the rooftops of Clarity Labs.

The attic floor shook from the force of whatever the bugbears were doing in our old bedrooms below us. It felt like a demolition crew had arrived. Our parents were gathered round the attic door, trying to plot our escape through the bedroom windows below if we could just drop down while the bugbears weren't looking, but I wasn't too excited about going down there again.

Suzie joined us at the window and pointed to the box of eucalyptus oil among the remnants of the Prius. "The eucalyptus oil worked like catnip on the peeves. Maybe it will do the same on the bugbears." But as she was talking about eucalyptus oil, I was thinking about the Buzz-Off Pest Control van that was still parked on the street. The back door hung open, and I could see all the fumigation equipment was still inside. And suddenly an idea struck. "If we can lure the bugbears back to Clarity Labs . . ." I started to say as Lucy quickly caught on. "Then maybe that Dr Zanker freakazoid has some other biological weapon to destroy them!" she finished.

The floor shook again and the far wall of the attic

suddenly sank, like the house was being destabilised below us. I grabbed the digital photo frame from Asking Peeve and threw it at the window, hoping to break it. But I only broke the frame, which skidded across the floor towards our parents, just as a bugbear arm punched up through the floor, groping around and grabbing the broken memories before falling back down, pulling a huge chunk of the floor with it.

"Stand back," said Lucy, wielding a pair of her old soccer trophies. She tossed one at the window, which smashed straight through, and then used the other to clear the broken glass from the edges.

"It's still too small!" Lucy said, just as a bugbear bashed up through the floor at our feet, knocking me back and tearing a chunk of wall below the window out.

I sat up and saw Lucy and Suzie still safe across from me, but then I felt a breeze. The bugbear had actually done us a favour and made the window big enough to escape through. "Go!" screamed Dad from the other side of the attic. Our parents were trying to get to us, but bugbear legs and tongues were popping up through the floor like a horrific Whac-A-Mole game.

Lucy slid out of the window hole first. "Come on!" she yelled.

But I'm terrified of heights, like so many other things, and I was too scared to move. Suzie hurried after Lucy, sliding out onto the pitched roof of the house. I peeked out and could see them clinging to the shingles, feet braced on the gutters. My whole body was shaking. I turned back and saw a bugbear rip the floor down over my old bedroom, leaving a pair of exposed beams crossing the expanse between my parents and me. Mom and Dad started to move across one and Brad and Chad stepped out on the other, performing a daredevil feat I was grateful I didn't have to do.

A bugbear grabbed an exposed beam and tried to pull itself up, but Mom knocked it off by kicking a teetering box of our memories down into its frothing mouth. But the house shook again, sending all four parents wobbling and grasping for balance. From what I could see through the floor that no longer existed, two bugbears seemed to be on parent patrol and the others seemed to be trying to destroy the very foundations of this house so we'd all fall down to their level.

That's when a little voice next to me piped up to ask, "How can I help?"

I looked down to see Asking Peeve against the wall

next to me. The little guy looked so eager to help. And honestly, we needed it. "Can you distract the bugbears long enough for us to escape?" I asked in desperation. The little peeve looked down at the bugbears below, clearly thinking about it, and then it smiled and nodded and struggled and strained to form an answer without asking a question. "Yes . . . I . . . can," it said with the involuntary raised inflection of a question but determined face of an answer.

I couldn't help it. I reached over to Asking Peeve and ruffled its furry little head like I would have done to a family dog, if Mom and Dad had ever let me get one. (Lucy is allergic to dogs and cats, so having a pet was never really an option, even when my therapist said it would be good for me.) And I don't know if it was just the adrenaline pumping through my body or if it was seeing this tiny little creature ready to overcome its own limitations to help out, but I suddenly had the courage to pull myself free from the wall and climb through the window hole.

As I slid out onto the sloping shingles of the roof, I could see a bugbear's tongue catch Brad by the ankle. He fell hard, holding tight to the beam and engaging all his yoga core strength to keep from being pulled towards the gooey mouth waiting to swallow him whole below. "Dad!" screamed Suzie from next to me on the roof. That's when Asking Peeve jumped into action, clambering over the backs of Dad and Chad as they struggled to pull Brad free, and jumping through the hole in the floor down into what used to be my bedroom. It landed with a gushy thud on the bugbear's face, which caused it to *ROAR* and release Brad, who was pulled to safety.

"Think you can eat me?" taunted Asking Peeve. "What are you waiting for?"

The two bugbears that were attacking our parents must have lumbered off after it, because the next thing I knew, Mom and Dad and Brad and Chad were sliding past me down the roof. Someone grabbed onto me in panic and I slid down the roof and was suddenly hanging from the gutter, just between two bedroom windows. When I dared to open my eyes, I saw the others shimmying down the porch roof and climbing to the ground below. Before I could think, the other two bugbears busted holes in the exterior wall on either side of me.

Asking Peeve bounced across one bugbear's head and down its arm before scrambling up and over my head and onto the other bugbear. "Why are you so mean?" it asked as it lured the bugbears away from me on a chase through the upstairs rooms of the house. The bugbears clearly wanted to eat peeves more than they wanted to eat people. I felt bad leaving Asking Peeve all alone, but I didn't see any other choice.

"Slim, let's go! Now," Mom yelled from down in the front yard. Lucy and the Minkles were right next to her. I wanted to let go, but my vision blurred with vertigo and I shut my eyes tight. "It's okay, Slim. I've got you." I opened my eyes and saw Dad was climbing back onto the porch roof below. "Just let go," he added as a bugbear leg smashed through my parents' old bedroom window and swiped at me. That was enough incentive for me to do as I was told. I dropped onto the porch roof and slid down to the edge, where Dad was waiting. I heard Asking Peeve yell out, "Do I annoy you? Do I annoy you? Do I annoy you?" And apparently it did because the bugbear went back inside to chase after the peeve again.

Dad helped me swing down from the porch into Mom's arms below. He jumped down after me, and as we hurried away from danger, I looked back at our old house. The whole ground floor was nearly destroyed. There was a spine-tingling *CREAKING MOANING GROANING* sound and Mom turned in a fresh panic. "The house is going to collapse!" she shouted, grabbing me by the arm and pulling me off towards the relative safety of the Buzz-Off van. Suzie and Lucy grabbed the eucalyptus oil on the way, and we climbed through the extermination equipment in the back of the van just as the living-room wall collapsed into the yard.

Our home suddenly seemed like one of those doll's houses that my sister used to play with – the ones with flimsy walls and no front so you could see inside and move your dolls and furniture around. Except this doll's house was life-size and a bugbear stood in the middle of the living room, busily smashing out walls as it searched for Asking Peeve.

Chad hopped into the driver's seat of the Buzz-Off van and Dad sat next to him. Mom and Brad helped Suzie figure out how to jury-rig the fumigation device and load the eucalyptus oil in the back. Chad hot-wired the ignition with a penknife he pulled from his pocket. Dad and I exchanged a look like, "Whoa," but Chad just shook his head and said, "Don't ask."

"This is crazy. Why are we doing this? Why do we have to lure these things after us?!" asked Mom.

I shuffled back to them, looking off at the half-demolished house in which little Asking Peeve was taking on four giant monsters. Maybe even six if the basement bugbears had got loose.

"Because it's not enough to treat the symptoms," I said. "Not any more."

I crawled up next to Lucy as a bugbear smashed a hole through the exterior wall in her old room. "I always did want a window there," she quipped in a sort of shell-shocked tone. But I was busy looking for Asking Peeve. It hadn't been eaten – yet. I saw it pop its head out of the top of the crumbling chimney, but I also knew that it wouldn't be able to avoid the bugbears for ever on its own. "Come on, Asking. Get out of there!" I shouted.

Asking Peeve bounded across the top of the house with bugbears hot on its trail, causing another incredibly loud creaking sound. Chad revved the engine and looked back at us. "We ready?" Brad and Mom had the fumigation device loaded up with all the eucalyptus oil. "I hope so," said Brad as Lucy and I aimed the fumigation tubes out of the open back doors. Suzie hit the switch on the fumigation device as Chad drove the van down the street, pausing a safe distance from the house as a massive amount of eucalyptus oil diffused into the air.

I called out to Asking Peeve, "Come on! Let's go!" It slid down the last standing drainpipe onto the porch roof just as the eucalyptus oil hit its nostrils. Suddenly

Asking Peeve got super sedated and just sort of moseyed along the porch roof towards us.

"No, no, no! You have to hurry!" I shouted, but it was no use. Asking Peeve was heading our way, but it was super chill about it as four bugbears closed in.

Before they got to Asking Peeve, they caught the scent of the eucalyptus oil too. They all paused to breathe it in, confused by this new, alluring smell. They all turned towards the scent . . . towards the van . . . towards us. Just as Suzie suspected, it had the same effect on the bugbears as it did on the peeves. They all moved *en masse* in our direction, causing the porch roof to creak and crack and crash. The remaining front half of the house broke free, tipped forward, and collapsed on the front lawn like a boxer right after the knockout punch.

Asking Peeve practically air-surfed on a broken gutter until it hit the lawn, pitching the little blue fur ball up above a massive cloud of dust, where it caught the corners of the fumigation tent that fluttered free. It used it like a parachute and glided safely towards the ground until a gust of debris blasted Asking Peeve even higher into the air instead. The chilled-out peeve didn't even seem bothered. It caught another whiff of eucalyptus, smiled dopily, and just let go of the tent-chute. It plummeted to the ground, landing face-first with a SPLAT on the lawn. I almost ran out after it, but Mom held me back.

Four bugbears emerged from the destruction as Asking Peeve reinflated. It picked its head up from the grass, spat out a clump of dirt, and looked at me like it couldn't believe it was going to make it! Then it got another whiff of eucalyptus and it stood up like it didn't have a care in the world. And it wasn't alone. The four bugbears were also in the thrall of eucalyptus oil. One of them lazily rolled out its tongue, slapping around like it couldn't quite be bothered to put any serious effort into catching the last peeve but it still couldn't help but try.

"Look!" yelled Lucy, pointing to the rear portion of the house where the two other bugbears were crawling up the debris to escape the basement. They were so drawn to the eucalyptus scent that they walked right through the one remaining support beam to get to it, causing what was left of the house to come crumbling down.

The destruction blew forward in a cloud of dust, enveloping Asking Peeve just as that bugbear tongue was poised to snatch it up. "Nooooo!" I yelled, but it was too late. Only the bugbears emerged from that dust. And they were heading right for us.

"Go, go, go!" yelled Mom as the bugbears followed the eucalyptus trail towards us.

Chad hit the gas. Brad and Mom grabbed me and Lucy and Suzie, pulling us deeper into the van. But it was hardly a high-speed chase. Chad kept us just far enough ahead of the dazed bugbears to ensure their slow, steady pursuit.

All I could think about was poor little Asking Peeve. "It sacrificed itself to save the people it was born to annoy," I said softly.

Suzie sat next to me, looking off at the destruction we left behind and said, "Then make sure its sacrifice means something."

Up front, Dad turned round to confirm that we were safe. And I could see Mom blinking back tears next to me. She turned away from the wreck of our family home and looked back at Dad. I don't know what they were feeling, but he reached out and squeezed her shoulder and she touched his hand as he did. It was enough to remind me that we all still cared about each other, even if some of us couldn't stand to be around each other.

But the moment was short-lived; our problems were still chasing us. Chad took a corner hard and slowed down to make sure the bugbears could keep up. Out of the open back door, I could see the six of them lumbering after us, blissed out on the sweet scent of eucalyptus oil. They followed us right out of the neighbourhood.

The plan was working. The oil was like catnip. They couldn't get enough. And then I realised it might have worked too well. Another bugbear broke away from smashing into a neighbour's house to join the chase. Then another one bounded out of the nearby woods, dropping a bathrobe-clad lady who didn't pause to wonder why. She scrambled to her feet and ran away down the empty streets. Either people were hiding or the bugbears had got them. As we passed an abandoned ambulance, still flashing its lights, we Pied Pipered another bugbear. And I swear through its blackish-purple body, I could see the outline of a human body stuck inside. It looked like the incessant sniffler, Otis Miller. He was a jerk, sure, but even I knew no one deserved that fate.

But the bugbear that ate him quickly got lost in the crowd. Suddenly, there were ten bugbears in pursuit. Then twelve. Then twenty. The eucalyptus oil was drawing them to us from all over town like rats to stinky cheese.

As we turned onto Main Street, navigating round

all the abandoned cars and general wreckage, there were now too many bugbears on our tail to count. "We need to catch them all," said Lucy. "Like Pokémon." She was right. If we had any hope of stopping this nightmare, we had to get all of these bugbears back to Clarity Labs. And if Dr Zanker couldn't kill them, then at least he'd go down with us. There'd be no PVZ 2.0 if we could help it.

But as we made the slow roll towards the lab, a sputter from the fumigation device made me realise our eucalyptus oil supply was dwindling fast, and I started to wonder if we were leading the bugbears towards their doom – or our own.

CHAPTER 15

THE BURNING SENSATION

I was too busy spraying the bugbears with eucalyptus oil to see the smoke. It wasn't until we were almost at the front gates to Clarity Labs that I started to smell it.

"That's not good," Dad said from the passenger side front seat. I turned to sneak a peek through the windshield. Clarity Labs looked like a giant version of the roaring campfires we used to make at Big Moose Lake.

Chad slowed the van as we approached the burning building. The heat was so strong we couldn't have got very close if we'd dared. I guess Pyro Peeve got what it wanted after all.

"What should we do now?" asked Chad, taking his foot off the gas a shade too much. A bugbear caught up with us and grabbed the fumigation tube out of Lucy's hand. It stuffed its face in the opening and inhaled the eucalyptus oil as deeply as possible.

"Don't slow down! Don't slow down!" she yelled. Chad hit the gas hard, sending me and Lucy sprawling backwards, but also pulling the tube away from the bugbear.

"The lab is toast," said Dad, "Zanker is long gone. One way or another."

"And we will be too if we don't find another solution soon," I added.

"We're running out of eucalyptus oil," Suzie chimed in as the fumigation device started to sputter again.

Chad sped away from the building, tyres squealing, hundreds of bugbears close behind in lumbering pursuit. "Pauline Salt is too resourceful to go down with the lab," assured Dad. "And she needs Dr Zanker. He's the only person who might know how to stop any of this, and she'll follow him anywhere, if only to protect the damn company."

"Where would they go?" asked Mom.

"He wanted to take us to his *real* lab!" I remembered. "That has to be Plum Island!"

As we headed down the coast, Lucy pointed excitedly to the docks down in the distance. "The ferry!" she shouted. "That's where it goes!"

I looked out at the abandoned ferry. The gate to the dock was open, and the ferry was anchored with its ramp down so we could drive this van right up onto it.

"She's right!" I agreed. "If that's where Zanker first made PVZ, maybe there's something on the island that can stop it. And maybe these bugbears don't know how to swim!" I added, hoping to take the Pied Piper portion of our evening to its logical conclusion by drowning all the monsters that were after us.

Lucy smiled at me; for once, my sister and I were totally on the same page.

The fumigation device sputtered out for good and the scent of eucalyptus started to fade. One bugbear *ROARED*. Then they all did.

Chad floored it, jumping the kerb and bounding across the grass divides in the ferry parking lot, tossing us all around inside the van before he smashed through the security booth. This wasn't a public ferry; it was actually a government ferry that apparently only serviced employees of the Plum Island Animal Disease Centre. At least that's what I gathered from the pieces of the sign we had just smashed through.

Chad hit the brakes as we boarded the ferry and fishtailed, skidding to a stop inches short of going over the bow. I followed Lucy and clambered out of the van.

"That was . . . impressive," Dad said to Chad as he rushed to the loading area, hitting a button that raised the ramp on the ferry. Brad and Mom pulled the ropes off the moorings. And Chad ran to the helm and started the engine. Suzie, Lucy and I stood at the railing and watched the bugbears crash into each other at the edge of the dock as the ferry jerked to life and pulled away.

I should have been thrilled that we were getting away, but I was too disturbed by what was happening with the bugbears. They weren't just colliding with each other; they were *combining* with each other. Hundreds of them. One after another, they stopped short at the water and ploughed into each other. Their gooey, gummy, six-legged bodies combined like a series of action figures that you could lock together to create a mega-monster figure. It was just like the panic monster I saw when my whole class turned on me after the booger incident – except this was a million times worse because it was real and wanted to eat me. Whatever hopes I had that the bugbears would just follow us into the water and drown were gone. Instead, they were transforming into something far, far worse – a massive, hideous, angry beast.

"What's happening to them?" asked Lucy in a trembling voice.

It was another stage. Another evolution. And, once again, it felt strangely familiar. And I knew from experience it would be so much worse and *so* much harder to stop than anything that came before it. I stared in horror, trying to put that feeling into words that everyone else might understand.

"Remember the road trips to Big Moose Lake?" I asked without taking my eyes off the mega-monster forming on the shore. "You were in a bad mood, I was in a bad mood, and we were all stuck in a car in bad moods for hours with nowhere else to go and nothing to distract us but our own irritation at everyone else. Eventually we didn't even remember what we were so angry and annoyed about, but it didn't matter. With that much negativity in such a small space, everything we said and did just made things worse. Like we could all explode at any second. The whole thing was a total nightmare."

Lucy nodded, eyes so wide in fear I thought they might pop out.

"That's what's happening to them," I said, nodding to the bugbears forming a new creature on the shore. "That's stage three," I added as Mom and Dad and Brad and Suzie stood behind me, trying to make sense of the fast-mutating monster. And then I spat out the only word I could think of to describe it. "Meet . . . the SPITE!"

CHAPTER 16

THE SOUND AND FURY

There was no preparing any of us for how terrifying the spite actually was. Bugbear legs protruded out of its massive body at odd angles. It had a sinister-looking, insectlike face and it had grown taller than several school buses before it flopped over. I thought it might have grown too big for itself but then it began to move like a monster-centipede straight out of a schlocky horror movie. But not even an IMAX 3-D film could have captured the scope of this thing. Or the fear it made me feel.

The spite skittered back and forth on the water's edge. It wanted to come after us but didn't seem to be able to figure out how to do so. It rose up on its hind legs and screeched so loudly that it actually caused the ferry to rock. Dad leaned on the railing, staring in disbelief across the dark, moonlit sound at the newly formed spite. "All-natural behaviour-modifying treatment, my butt," he said, except he used a different word for "butt".

"It might not be natural, but it has definitely modified our behaviour," Lucy noted.

As I watched the spite grow angrier, I had the sudden, horrible premonition that its next move would be to retreat back to town and go on a rampage there. More innocent people would be hurt, or even killed. Suzie must have been thinking the same thing because she said, "They were quarantining the town. Blocking the roads. Nobody is getting out."

"Maybe the CDC people can stop it?" suggested Lucy. "Maybe they'll call in the army?"

I had to remind her: "Only people who have been exposed to PVZ can see any of these things. Even if the army showed up, they can't fight what they can't see."

Suzie gulped in horror. "There's no stopping that thing. The whole town is doomed."

The spite screeched furiously one more time before suddenly plunging into the deep, dark water to come after the ferry. "Or maybe just us," I said in dismay.

A tense moment passed before the spite resurfaced. It was big enough to stand on the bottom of the sound. It was moving slowly, but it was clearly determined. And it was gaining on us. But as we puttered out into the deepest parts of the water, the spite wasn't tall enough to keep its head above the surface. It was thrashing its comparably tiny legs, gasping for air, trying to swim. It seemed panicked and furious, but it refused to give up and turn back. And somewhere in the middle of the sound, it finally sank into the deep, dark depths below.

"Is that it?" asked Lucy as we saw a few final bubbles float up to the surface. I stared hard at the water churning behind the ferry, fully expecting that horror-movie moment when the spite bursts out and eats us all, but it never came. I really didn't know what to say. "I hope so," was the best I could offer as we all turned away from the railing.

We gathered at the bridge of the ferry and filled Chad in on the details of the spite.

"It was terrifying," said Brad.

"But it's dead, right?" asked Chad, uncertain, but hopeful. None of us could say for sure. And we were all too exhausted, both physically and emotionally, to consider any other alternative. I slumped down on the floor, tired and done.

"My therapist always tells me we have to face the monsters we create," I said. "Except I don't think she meant like, real actual monster-monsters. So we overshot a little there."

As the ferry chugged along into the dark night without anything chasing us, I felt like I could relax for the first time all day. That is, until Brad said, "We might want to talk about those figurative monsters now." Suzie rolled her eyes with an audible groan, but Brad continued regardless. "Suzie, I think your father and I might be a little overzealous in our pursuit of a healthy, balanced life. You know we're not the typical family in this town. Hell, we're practically a walking advertisement for diversity. It's easy to succumb to insecurities because it feels like we're judged for being different."

Chad turned away from the helm to reassure her as well. "We just want to make sure you have as little negativity in your life as possible. But we never want you to pretend you don't feel the things you feel. That's the opposite of who we are. Your dad and I, of all people, know how unhealthy it is to try to be something you're not."

Brad pulled her close and added, "Balance involves all of our feelings. Being mindful doesn't mean ignoring the negative thoughts; it just means not letting them control you."

Suzie seemed a little overwhelmed by the whole thing and simply hugged both of her dads. "I'm sorry. I should have told you how I felt," she said.

"We love you," said Brad.

"You can always tell us anything," added Chad as he gave them both a kiss. It was a really sweet scene until Lucy cut in to say "Barf," and then pretended to gag.

"Lucy!" chided Mom. "Come here."

Lucy's eyes went wide as Mom pulled her close.

Dad turned to us and stuttered a bit before clearing his throat and admitting, "Things have been hard. For a while now. I know I've been . . . distant. And your mother and I . . . aren't doing a great job. It hasn't been fair to either of you."

And to my surprise, Mom agreed with Dad. "We need to get our poop together," she said, except she actually used Dad's favourite word. "Our family didn't function before, but we haven't done much to make the new dynamic any better." She paused as if she were fighting the urge to own the blame, to accept her own faults. "It's not a project I can manage alone," she admitted. "Things went so much better today when we all worked together."

Dad nodded in agreement. "And when we actually listened to each other," he added with an apologetic half smile.

Mom half smiled back. "Things have changed, but we're still a team. We're still a family. We always will be." And then they stood there expectantly, as if they were waiting for Lucy or me to do something. It was awkward. Mom and Dad exchanged a look, like they should keep going. "We all need to stop acting out," added Mom. But we still just stood there.

"And . . . try to help each other instead of bothering each other," Dad continued.

Lucy shot me a look like we should stop them before this moment got even weirder and said, "I've already made it pretty clear that I feel neglected. This part's on you."

So I was on the spot – and I'm not very good at being on the spot. But this time, I just took a deep breath, stood up, and finally spoke some truth. "I just wish maybe you could spend less time trying to fix me and more time trying to understand me."

Mom and Dad looked equal parts heartbroken and guilty. "Honey, we don't want to 'fix' you; we just want to support you," said Mom. "Like the Minkles said, we all need balance, and sometimes we need help finding it."

Dad nodded. "I'm . . . I'm sorry if we've pushed you in the wrong ways," he said. "If today is any indication of what you go through on a regular basis, I'd say we understand a lot better now."

"You're stronger than you know," added Mom,

getting really emotional. "We wouldn't have got away without your quick thinking."

"And we just love you so much," choked out Dad as he tried not to cry.

It was nice to hear, but it felt weird to be talking like this. And they were both all teary-eyed, which was making me all teary-eyed, and I really didn't want to cry in front of Suzie. Judging by Lucy's face, we both wanted the moment to be over. "For crying out loud, just hug it out," said Brad. And so we all did – a big, awkward, family hug – the kind that reminded me we really are in this together.

A loud beeping came from the steering console to notify us that we were approaching our destination: Plum Island. We let go of our hug and turned to face the oncoming harbour.

At first it looked dark and ominous on the horizon, but as the island came into moonlit view, I was surprised to see how unassuming it was. I suppose I was expecting it to be more of a volcano-ridden, sinister-seeming, mad scientist's lair. But Plum Island wasn't very big, and it was covered in mossy trees and nondescript, warehouse-style buildings. But even if it didn't have a skull-shaped cove to welcome us, there was still something a little off about it.

"It looks too normal," said Lucy, voicing my exact thought.

"What are we even doing here? It's over, right? The spite drowned," said Suzie.

"We need to know for sure," I said as Chad docked the ferry.

"And at least we know we'll be safe here," Dad said as a crew of armed security forces descended upon us. At first, I was thrilled. I thought they'd come to protect us. But when they surrounded us, guns pointed, I knew the opposite was true.

CHAPTER 17

THE RISING

I had my hands up before they even told us to put them in the air. Chad and Brad were trying to explain that we'd come in peace, when a serious-looking, barrel-chested, stone-faced leader stepped forward and identified himself as General Esposito. "That's a stolen vessel and you are trespassing on government property," he started, before cocking his head to listen to an earpiece that was clearly giving him orders. He looked up, drawing my attention to the security cameras on the light poles above us as he nodded. "Understood," he said into the earpiece, then motioned his security detail towards us. "Bring them in."

The Plum Island Animal Disease Centre – it's a real mouthful to say, even if it isn't much to look at. We were marched into an unmarked building. The doors opened onto a generic lobby decorated with only an empty fish tank. We were herded down a grey hall that echoed our every footstep and into an empty room marked with a sheet of copy paper on which someone had written "containment". In it were two folding metal chairs and not much else. It was the second time I'd been quarantined today, which was two times too many.

"I really thought there would be more mad scientists and test tubes – and far fewer watercoolers," said Lucy. An old watercooler bubbled at that moment as if it were agreeing with her.

"Yeah, this really doesn't feel like a place where they develop biological weapons," I agreed.

"That's because it's not," a familiar voice cut in. We turned to see Pauline Salt *click-clack* into the room. She was cool, calm and composed despite her singed hair and soot-stained power suit. Clearly she barely escaped the fire at Clarity Labs. "If we let you in any further, you'd have to go through our decontamination process," she added. "It would involve a full-body scrubbing. You can thank me later."

"I see you survived the lab fire," said Dad in a tone that suggested he wasn't totally thrilled about that.

"Yes, apparently one of our lab technicians finds smoke to be particularly irritating. Her Pyro Peeve burned the place down. There were no fatalities, so we dodged a lawsuit there," informed Ms Salt. "After you fled, Dr Zanker and I were also infected with peeves.

Once they evolved into . . ." She trailed off, failing to find the word.

"Bugbears," I said.

"Bug . . . bears?" she repeated. All of us nodded as if this were the generally accepted scientific term and not just a name I assigned them on the fly. Pauline Salt moved forward accordingly. "When the . . . bugbears . . . developed, we took the corporate chopper and regrouped here to commence with damage control," she continued, blowing a stray hair out of her face before smoothing it back into her bun. "Clarity Labs is now ground zero for potential litigation," she said, directing her attention at Dad, "so we'll have to coordinate our stories if we're going to spin this right."

He just blinked at her, not comprehending. "There's no way I'm working for Clarity Labs any more. You know this, right?" She tilted her head up to avoid seeming like she had been caught off guard, even though she had clearly been caught off guard.

The door then opened and a very excited Dr Zanker hurried in, carrying sheaves of research. "I think I have it! There must have been an anomaly in the modified gene sequence of the PVZ amoebas," he rambled before looking up, surprised to see us. "Oh! You've come voluntarily?" he said, baffled. "How curious — but okay.

240

Let's get you to my lab and run some tests!" he exclaimed to entirely the wrong crowd.

"Your 'tests' destroyed our town and nearly killed us," said Mom in her most "Mom" tone.

"The bugbears ate up all the peeves and then morphed into—" I started to explain.

But Dr Zanker cut me off. "Bugbears?" he questioned. Then, upon quick consideration, he said, "Oh, yes. I see what you did there. It works on multiple levels."

"And that was before the spite even happened," I finished.

Dr Zanker's face went slack. "The . . . spite?" He looked at Pauline Salt, who once again tilted her head up to avoid seeming like she had been caught off guard, even though she had clearly been caught off guard.

"You don't know about the spite yet, do you?" I asked, and they both stared at me blankly. "Stage three? The spite? All the bugbears mashed together and formed this mega-monster centipede-looking thing that's just, like, pure . . . rage."

"I missed the spite?" Dr Zanker said, the same way a little kid might react if they found out they missed Santa Claus.

"Um, yeah, poor you!" said Suzie sarcastically.

Lucy chimed in with, "It jumped in the ocean and tried to chase us, but drowned."

"Extraordinary," wasn't the phrase any of us would think to use to describe our near-death experience, but that's exactly what Dr Zanker said.

"We didn't come here to pat you on the back for making an evolving monster," said Dad in the most "Dad" tone possible. "We came here for answers. To make sure this is over. To make sure we, and all the other people who have been affected by PVZ, are okay," he finished.

"Are we even safe here now?" asked Chad.

Pauline Salt stepped forward and spoke to us like she was reading off a press release: "The Plum Island Animal Disease Centre is a research facility overseen by the US Department of Agriculture, but the island and overall programme are actually controlled by Homeland Security. We're safe as long as you haven't brought any more complications with you," she explained. "The one saving grace in all of this is that the only way to see the peeves or the bugbears, or even this spite that you speak of, I'm assuming, is to have been exposed to PVZ in the first place. No one apart from those who were exposed can see the things we've experienced, so that makes this all a bit . . . cleaner."

Mom's jaw almost hit the floor at how single-minded Ms Salt could be. "Clean?" she said. "The whole town is a disaster zone!"

"How do we know it's over? Or that it won't happen again?" asked Brad.

That's when Dr Zanker spoke up again, happy to talk about his work. "It appears that the spread of PVZ itself stops at the point when the afflicted sneezes out the final PVZ amoeba and it becomes a so-called bugbear," he said, referencing the stack of research he was still clutching. "Therefore, the contagion has ended. All other PVZ samples were either destroyed in the Clarity Labs fire or have been contained here for study." Then he pulled out a chart with all sorts of facts and figures and scientific jargon I couldn't understand. "There were only three stages of the original weaponised PVZ. Stage three should only happen if stage two has fully ended. And it should only happen once. So if the spite is dead, then it sounds like this situation is officially water under the bridge ... or the sound, so to speak."

"So we're okay? There will be no lasting effects beyond what's already happened?" asked Dad.

"PVZ was never designed to be permanent. As a weapon it was more of a 'shock and awe' scenario. And as a treatment, the effects were designed to be temporary," explained Dr Zanker.

"Think about it: how would we sustain the product sales if it were a one-time fix? You know as well as I do that return customers are what keep us afloat," added Pauline Salt in another tone-deaf appeal to the bottom line.

"So . . . we're free to go?" asked Chad.

"General Esposito will escort you back to the mainland," said Pauline Salt. "You can't expect me to let you leave in a stolen ferry. That would be highly unethical." And if she had any concept of how hypocritical that statement was, she didn't show it at all.

Dr Zanker tried to give us one last hard sell on prolonging this inadvertent experiment, but Pauline Salt silenced him with a stern look and two words: "Damage control".

"You'll be hearing from our attorney," Mom said to Pauline Salt as we left the room. But once we were in the hall, Mom saw Dad's confused look and shrugged. "She doesn't know it's our divorce attorney."

General Esposito and his security detail met us in the lobby and escorted us outside and past the ferry to another dock where one of their own boats was waiting.

A mist crawled over the water and settled onto land, giving me the chills. I couldn't quite shake how strange it was that this was over.

"Um, does this all seem a little too easy — or is it just my anxiety rising again?" I asked Suzie and Lucy.

"If it's your anxiety, I think I have it now too," said Suzie.

"What if the spite is just hanging out at the bottom of the ocean and waiting for us to let our guard down? What if it breeds? What if there end up being hundreds of them and they attack the whole world all at once? What if all of humanity is destroyed by our own monstrous feelings?" said Lucy in a thought spiral of her own. I stared at her, gape-mouthed, as my anxiety ratcheted up a dozen notches to full-blown paranoia.

"You know that whole speech Mom and Dad gave about listening to and helping each other? Let's start by not giving me any more panic attacks," I said.

Lucy shrugged. "Okay. Maybe there's nothing left to see here. Maybe it's really over."

But then the ocean exploded.

The soldiers had just crowded us out onto the dock when a massive wave crested and crashed on top of us. We were instantly soaked. And by the time I cleared my eyes, the spite had risen. It was covered in seaweed and, if it's possible, it looked even scarier than before.

"It's not over! It's *definitely* not over! It's panic time!" Lucy yelled as we stumbled back. The security detail hadn't been infected with PVZ, so they couldn't see or hear the spite. They had no idea where the giant wave came from. All they could have known was that they were soaked and there were weird patches of seaweed that seemed to float in midair. But the spite could definitely see the soldiers. It screeched loud enough to blow my hair back – and we didn't stick around to see what was coming next. We turned on our heels and ran faster than any of us had ever run before.

"Hey, where do you think you're going?" yelled General Esposito, trying to maintain some semblance of control over the situation.

I caught a glimpse over my shoulder as the spite swept a bunch of the security detail off the dock and out to sea. It then grabbed a soldier in its bugbear legs, passing it up, leg over leg, before swallowing the soldier whole. "Steinberg!" yelled General Esposito, but to no avail. I couldn't even imagine what that must have looked like to the soldiers who couldn't see the monster at all.

General Esposito ordered his team to draw their

weapons, but they didn't know what to shoot at. He radioed for backup, but he was having a tough time explaining what was going on. "Retreat!" shouted General Esposito to his soldiers instead. As they all caught up with us, he shouted, "What am I not seeing? What is happening?"

We took cover round the corner of the main building. "There's a mega-monster coming out of the sound," I told him, watching the spite the whole time. It was still slowly thrashing its way out of the water. "You can't see it because you haven't been exposed to PVZ, which absorbed our annoyances but also spawned a bunch of little monsters made out of them. Those monsters became bigger monsters and those bigger monsters combined into a mega-monster. That's what just swallowed Steinberg. Sorry." With the moon behind it, I could make out the shape of the soldier stuck inside the spite's gelatinous belly.

General Esposito looked at me in exactly the way you'd expect him to look at me. The story sounded nut-balls crazy. I knew that. And yet, everyone nodded in agreement.

"So . . . we're confronting invisible . . . feelings?" General Esposito said, removing his hat and running a hand through what little was left of his hair.

"If this weren't actually happening, we'd all totally agree with how insane that sounds," said Mom.

Brad chimed in with, "I'm usually in favour of confronting negative feelings in healthy, constructive ways, but right now, sir, you have to order your men to aim their weapons in that general direction and blow that giant glob of monstrous feelings back to whatever corner of hell it came from!"

Chad then added, "Otherwise we'll all be eaten alive too."

The spite fully emerged from the water and shook the seaweed off its shoulders. The dock splintered and collapsed from the spite's weight. It made its way onto the island, seemingly hellbent on destruction for destruction's sake. It smashed, crashed and thrashed anything in its path.

Dr Zanker and Pauline Salt came out of the building and stopped short at the sight of the fast-approaching spite. Ms Salt looked like she could see her entire career passing before her eyes. "This is going to be hard to spin," she said.

But Dr Zanker was in awe of this new stage of his creation. "It's an evolutionary marvel," he whispered under his breath. "It's a *revolutionary* marvel!" he practically shouted, inadvertently drawing the spite's attention. It *ROARED* directly at us.

General Esposito looked at them both, utterly confused. "Ma'am, sir, what am I looking at here? How do we stop this?" His remaining team was right behind him, their weapons aimed every which way, but all that manpower was no good since none of them could actually see the spite.

Pauline Salt apparently realised that first. As General Esposito opened fire in the general direction of the monster, she ran away. The spite lashed out at the security detail, knocking a bunch of them off their feet and into the air. They crashed down at our feet.

"Is anyone else really starting to miss their little peeves?" I said, frozen in fear again. Mom grabbed me by the shirt collar, and we all followed Pauline Salt's lead and fled.

General Esposito and his men unleashed another round of ammo in the general direction of the invisible spite. The *pop pop pop pop pop* of gunshots was so much louder than movies and video games had me believe. I flinched at every shot that rang out. But they got quieter and quieter – and then I heard General Esposito scream, and the gunshots ended completely. The spite had gobbled up our only hope of actual protection.

Pauline Salt beat us to the parking lot and hopped into an idling army jeep. "Wait for us!" shouted Dad, but Ms Salt peeled away, not even slowing down to let Dr Zanker jump in with her. She skidded around the building at top speed, but just before she jumped the kerb out of the lot, the spite smashed through the building and blocked the road. Her jeep crashed into it, bounced off its gummy flesh, and then spun around, tossing her out of the doorless sides as it rolled away. She scrambled up and started run-limping back our way, screaming for help. But we were too far away. We could only watch as the spite bent over, grabbed her by the modern-cut blazer, and swallowed her in a single gulp. Her shoes *click-clacked* on the pavement one last time when the spite spat them out.

"I think it's time to end this experiment before this experiment ends me," said Dr Zanker as if he finally realised his creation was out of control and that he was in danger.

Chad ran for the still-moving jeep, proving his stuntman credibility by leaping up into the driver's seat in a single bound. He yelled to us to hurry up and we all crammed in. With the spite in pursuit, Dr Zanker pointed Chad down a wooded access road. Suzie and I were right at the back, legs dangling out, facing the spite, which could move pretty fast for something its size. Chad took a hard turn, squishing me into Suzie, and I'm not sure who instigated it, but after the turn, she was holding my hand, which was a whole different kind of terrifying.

"How do we stop it?" yelled Mom.

"The best way to overcome spitefulness is mindfulness, positivity and compassion," Brad spat out in a panic before Chad cut him off by saying, "None of which is going to be particularly helpful right now! Where am I going?!"

Dr Zanker directed him down another wooded pass, temporarily losing the spite.

"This island is run by the military and mad scientists! There has to be something here to fight this thing!" shouted Lucy.

That's when Dr Zanker shouted, "She's right. STOP!"

Chad slammed on the brakes, practically giving us all whiplash. But Dr Zanker was out of the vehicle before it fully stopped. He ran for an abandoned-looking building that could have been the "before" picture in one of Mom's renovation projects.

"Follow him!" Brad yelled.

We all jumped out of the jeep and I completely gave in to the flight part of my fight-or-flight instincts.

"Just because the biological weapons programme was officially defunded, doesn't mean it's actually gone!" shouted Dr Zanker over his shoulder as he pulled out a security card, swiped it to open a hidden panel, and keyed in a seven-digit code. A secret door opened in the wall next to the actual door. Dr Zanker disappeared inside and the door closed behind him a beat before I got there.

Dad caught up and banged his fists on the door while Mom tried to open the panel in vain. It wouldn't open without a security card.

We were trapped outside, and I could hear the growling rumble of the spite getting closer. It stepped into the far end of the clearing, and when it spotted us, the growling rumble turned into an earsplitting *SCREECH*.

The spite reared up to its full, towering height, blotting out the moon, casting us into near-complete darkness. I always feared my uncontrollable feelings would one day be the end of me, but I never imagined I'd be dying like this.

I never imagined my anxieties would literally eat me alive.

CHAPTER 18

THE PANIC ATTACK

The spite towered over us. Its body was gelatinous, like the bugbears that formed it, and with the moonlight filtering through it, we could make out the silhouettes of all the people and peeves it had gobbled up. The spite let out a *SCREECH* so loud I had to grab on to Suzie to keep from being knocked over.

Chad and Brad started banging where the secret door disappeared, screaming, "Let us in! Let us in!" But Dr Zanker either couldn't hear or didn't care. Lucy stepped past me, pushed her way through to the hidden panel, and pulled a stack of security cards from her pocket.

"Where did you get those?" asked Mom.

"I . . . borrowed them," Lucy replied guiltily before turning away to swipe one card after another in the hope of finding one with the right security clearance. I let go of Suzie and smiled nervously before the spite crashed down onto its front legs, shaking the earth and nearly causing us all to fall over again.

Lucy tried the cards as fast as possible. Swipe. Fail. *BUZZ*. Swipe. Fail. *BUZZ*. Each card took a second or two to process and the spite was skittering across the clearing, straight for its next meal. Lucy kept swiping and the spite kept charging. I swear I saw it lick its lips – if it even had lips. And then . . . swipe – DING! A card finally worked!

"But what about the code?" Chad yelped. That's when I stepped in and, without thinking twice, plugged in the same seven digits Zanker had used.

The secret door slid open and we all tumbled through just as the spite crashed into the now closed door with a sickly slurp. As we all caught our breath, I thanked Lucy for saving us, but she was the one who was amazed. "How'd you know the code?"

"The weird part about anxiety is that I remember things. Mostly I can't forget things. This time I just sort of remembered how Dr Zanker's fingers moved."

She nodded, impressed, and said, "You're the best biological weapon a little sister could ever want."

Mom looked at Lucy and, in that special "Mom" tone of hers, said, "We're going to talk about this 'borrowing' thing later." But then we heard the spite thrashing and crashing outside with a renewed desperation. It wanted to get into the building badly.

"But we have more pressing things to worry about right now," she added.

I looked around and noticed we were in a small metal-walled room. It was an elevator. There was another security panel on the far wall. Lucy looked at me uncertainly, and I sort of shrugged. "Only one way to find out where this goes." Lucy swiped the card that got us in, and the panel lit up with the number 257. The elevator started to move down. We were going underground – way underground.

The world's longest, quietest thirty seconds later, the elevator came to a stop and the door opened on a long, cavernous tunnel lit only by the flickering overhead lights. "And here I thought this day couldn't get any freakier," said Suzie as we stepped out of the elevator. And as soon as the elevator closed behind us, three ominous *bangs* echoed out as the lights shut off, leaving us in the dark.

That's when we all heard the distant, tinny sounds of an old-timey song playing. Some spooky lady's voice crooning about how love is strange and not a game or something. It was innocent enough, I suppose, but under the circumstances, it sent shivers down my spine.

Mom recognised the song because she turned to

Brad and Chad and said, "*Dirty Dancing?*" And Suzie's parents both nodded. I think they were as creeped out as I was.

"Follow that music," I said, surprising myself with my sudden willingness to go towards the unknown. Dad led the way as we moved, single file, down the dark hall. Every sound, every breath, echoed in the dark. I held on to someone's belt. I wasn't sure whose.

"There's a light at the end of the tunnel," said Brad.

"It's not a good time for cheesy platitudes, Dad," whispered Suzie, but then we finally felt our way round a corner and saw what Brad was talking about. A bit of light was coming through a narrow, wire-latticed set of windows in the double doors ahead. "Oh, sorry," said Suzie, shrugging.

We pushed through the doors, stopping a step inside to let our eyes adjust to the light. The tinny music was louder now. Clearer too. Coming from speakers across the room. It was a duet – a love song between the spooky lady and her lover boy.

And if the scene didn't seem nuts before, now it seemed utterly surreal – the fictional mad scientist's lab I had imagined Plum Island would be had suddenly materialised into my life. "Yeah, this makes more sense," said Lucy.

The room was decked out in cold steel. Everything was reflective and it was too brightly lit. The cavernous space was arranged with impeccably organised chaos. Chemical vials and test tubes were surrounded by loose wires and surgical equipment. Beeping, pulsing screens stood in long rows next to high-tech tables piled with computer parts and robotic assistance arms that moved on their own.

"I used to think I liked modern design," said Mom, "but I'm re-evaluating a lot of things today."

The walls featured darkened glass enclosures that lit up as I walked past them. There were deranged lab rats, something that looked like a massive mutant tick, and a collection of wormy things with retractable tentacles that still haunt my nightmares.

"Look," said Lucy. She was pointing at computer screens connected to microscopes that were analysing some sort of substance with various multicoloured imaging techniques. There were little oblong shapes moving around.

"Single-cell amoebas," said Suzie, "like Mr Schwartz taught us about in science. It's how life began." She was right. I got the same lesson on evolution.

"It evolved from simple to complex," I added as I looked around at this bizarre room. Before I could even start to guess what it all meant, a *SWOOSHING*, *THUNKING* noise drew my attention. Across the room, Dr Zanker was opening and closing various drawers as he shimmied from one end of a workstation to another, his back to us, dancing around and singing along to the old-timey love song. I grimaced at his awkward, inappropriate hip movements.

"Ew," Lucy said, pointing at him. "Is he . . . dirty dancing?"

Dr Zanker spun to face us, a vial containing a noxious-looking liquid in one hand and a high-tech, rifle-size dart gun in the other. He closed his eyes, letting the song fade out before popping the vial into a dart and using the tip to hit a button that turned the music off. "Nothing quite like a golden oldie to soothe the soul, don't you think?" he said as he snapped the dart into the gun. "You aren't supposed to be here," he added, pointing the dart gun at my father.

"Pretty sure we could say that about a lot of things today," answered Dad. "Now point that thing somewhere else."

Dr Zanker looked at him in confusion for a moment, and then looked at the dart gun, realising it was aimed at us. He shook his head with an uneasy smile, saying, "Oh no. This isn't for you. It's for that," he said, pointing up, as if all the way to ground level where the spite was probably still rampaging. "I think this experiment has run its course for now," he concluded in a disturbingly casual manner. As if this had all been a pretty standard day in the lab of life.

"You said you couldn't cure PVZ because PVZ *was* the cure," I said.

"This," he said, stroking the noxious-looking vial loaded in the dart gun, "isn't technically a cure, per se; it's more of a fail-safe."

Once again, the vein in Dad's forehead looked like it might explode. "Using different words doesn't make you any less of a liar!" he shouted. "If that could have stopped this disaster, you should have used it – A LOT SOONER!"

Dr Zanker looked a little chastised, but he mostly looked like he was feeling sorry for himself. "You don't understand what it's like working for decades on a project only to see it shut down before you ever find out what you're really capable of accomplishing," he said, growing more impassioned and desperate.

But then Mom flipped her lid. "And *you* don't understand what it's like having kids," she countered, "wanting to make sure THEY aren't shut down before we find out what *they're* really capable of accomplishing!"

259

Dr Zanker scoffed. "I understand more than you know," he said, pulling out a little spray bottle of PVZ. "This is my baby. It's not perfect, but now there's an entirely new species out there and I created it! Don't you see how amazing that is?"

"There are living things in that anti-anxiety treatment?!" asked Chad, creeped out.

"And there's live bacteria in your yoghurt," responded Dr Zanker as if it were all the same thing.

"My Go-Gurt doesn't turn into monsters!" I shouted. "It's a little different!"

Dr Zanker considered that a moment and conceded. "Well. Yes. I did apply some genetic alterations to those little amoebas," he admitted. Then he caught himself. "I'm really not supposed to talk about this," he said, as if he might actually stop. "But I think we're past the point of formalities, don't you?" he continued with an eager smile.

"Are you actually going to give us an evil monologue right now?" I asked.

"It's not evil," he countered. "It's science. Science can't be good or evil; it's just facts. Discoveries. How you use them is what determines whether they're good or evil."

"And making a biological weapon that drives people crazy isn't evil?" asked Lucy.

260

"Well, that's debatable," Dr Zanker argued. "And I only made it. I never used it." A statement that was met with deadpan stares all around, prompting him to realise: "Until now, but this was an accident — a glorious, ground-breaking accident."

He wandered the lab, almost like he was giving us the grand tour. "The original PVZ was an airborne weapon, developed here in Lab 257. It was meant to be purely psychoactive. The intention was to amplify an enemy's perceived irritations in a hallucinatory manner. Then a larger sense of animosity and anger would feed on those irritations before culminating in a singular, all-consuming need to destroy everything around them, thereby turning our enemies on each other in a destructive fashion."

"That's insane," I said.

"The government agreed," he bemoaned. "They shut down the programme. But with a little re-engineering and some genetic tweaks at Clarity Labs, I realised the formula that was intended to amplify irritation could be used to absorb and dispose of it instead. In theory, that is. They really should have let me run human trials in a controlled setting. I never could have predicted the amoebas would become sentient and evolve into—"

"A giant people-eating monster!" interrupted Brad. "Stop talking and start killing it!"

Dr Zanker dropped his head in frustration. "That's exactly what I was about to do when you came down here," he whined as he headed to the door in a huff, like his mom had just told him to clean his room the moment he'd hit a new level on his favourite video game.

It was a far more anticlimactic moment than I'd been taught to expect from every final face-off with every super-villain in every movie I'd ever seen. "After this is over, you should probably seek professional help – in or out of jail," added Chad. He had a point. As unbelievable as everything had been leading up to this moment, the reality was that Dr Zanker wasn't a super-villain at all. He was a misguided scientist who probably has some undiagnosed mental issues that a good therapist would have a field day evaluating. For maybe the first time ever, my problems felt pretty tame. They may have caused me no small share of stress and heartache, but at least my issues didn't lead to mass destruction, serious injuries and who knows how many possible deaths.

We followed Dr Zanker down the hall to the elevator. "Shouldn't we have weapons too?" I asked.

"This is the only dose, so I'll handle it," he said with a confidence that was undermined by his fumbling, futile search for his security card. Lucy reached out and swiped her own security card at the elevator scan pad, opening the door. He snatched the card away from her and stepped aside, ushering the rest of us in. We hesitated, having been left behind by him before. Dr Zanker rolled his eyes. "Fine," he said and got in the elevator first. "Happy now?"

We crammed into the elevator, and Dr Zanker swiped his card again, sending us up to the surface to face the spite. As we rose closer to ground level, we could hear it attacking the building. The elevator shook as hundreds of bugbear legs rampaged ruthlessly above us.

"So, um . . . what's the plan?" I swallowed and asked.

Dr Zanker cocked the dart gun loudly. "I'm going to administer the fail-safe, thereby concluding this unofficial, but utterly enlightening first human trial of PVZ."

The elevator *dinged*, the door slid open, and Dr Zanker stepped out into the night, dart gun at the ready. But the spite was gone. Dr Zanker looked around, confused. No sign of the mega-monster. Just darkness. Dr Zanker finally thought to look up just as the spite pounced down from the building's roof and gobbled him whole. The dart gun went skittering into the clearing. Lucy pounded the elevator's control panel, but without the right security card, it wasn't going anywhere.

Before any of us could make a run for it, the spite attacked the elevator. It thrashed back and forth and pulled the entire elevator right out of its shaft. Everything was a blur at that point. We were all screaming and holding on to the walls and the railings and each other, struggling to keep anyone from falling out of the open elevator door as the spite swung us around.

The swinging came to a jolting stop as the spite finally caught the elevator in its upper legs. My eyes were clenched tight and I could feel the cool night breeze. When I opened them, my world was upside down. I was dangling far below the open door. The blood rushed to my head as I swung wildly around by my ankle, which was held by Chad, who was now hanging from the edge of the elevator by his other fingertips. I was so close to the spite that I swear I could see Pauline Salt smiling smugly inside it. Chad swung me back up into the elevator just as it flipped again and he tumbled in after me.

"This is why I retired from stunt work!" yelled Chad as he gasped for breath.

"There's no escape!" cried Mom.

The elevator shifted and rattled as it was passed down the long line of bugbear legs towards the ground.

"Is it putting us down?" asked Suzie in a panic. But we stopped about halfway to the ground. Then the elevator tipped forward, the open door facing directly downward. We all braced ourselves, holding on to the railings and trying to grab a foothold on the edges next to the open door that gave us a clear view straight into the horrific abyss of the spite's open mouth.

"It's going to eat us!" I yelled, and the spite shook the elevator like we were the last candy Nerds in the box.

Dad fell first. He slipped. Mom tried to grab him, but he was too heavy for her to hold. "Dale!" yelled Mom, but the only answer she got was Dad's scream as he plummeted down into the spite's mouth below. And by trying to help Dad, with the elevator shaking and all, she lost her footing too. Chad threw his body across the door, grabbing the other side and catching Mom like a human hammock. "Don't look down! Don't look down!" said Chad, like an expert stunt coach. But Mom slipped off his body and was hanging on by his shirt. Brad held tightly to his husband's feet while Suzie and Lucy grabbed his hands.

But I pressed myself in a corner, unable to do anything but shake in terror.

The spite wasn't satisfied. It screeched and shook the elevator even harder. I tumbled and cracked my back against the security panel next to the open door, but managed to grab the railing again. I looked over to see Brad doing his best to keep Suzie and Lucy safe by pinning them against the far wall, but Mom and Chad were gone, their screams silenced as the spite swallowed them too. Then it gave us another hard shake and Brad slipped and plummeted out of the door. I watched as he fell soundlessly into the spite's mouth. Suzie screamed and tried to go after him, but Lucy pulled her back and they both fell on their butts on the other side of the door.

The elevator shook and turned over again. Now the floor was the floor once more and Lucy and Suzie and I slid down opposite walls. I pushed myself back against my wall, staring across at Lucy and Suzie, gasping for breath. "What do we do?" yelled Lucy just as the elevator shook violently.

I held the railing on my side, but Lucy and Suzie slid up their wall, hit the ceiling, and then fell straight down through the open door as the elevator tilted again. I clenched my eyes, expecting to hear the spite swallowing them, but their screams didn't fade off with distance. I reluctantly opened my eyes and saw Suzie's hands gripping the edge of the elevator door. Paralysed with fear, I stretched my neck just enough to see Lucy swinging from Suzie's feet, just inches from the spite's open maw. If I didn't act, they would be goners.

I peeled one set of sweaty fingers off the railing and willed my body to inch closer to the edge while holding on with the other. The spite bellowed in frustration, blowing a nasty breeze of its foul breath up into the elevator. But still, somehow, I managed to grab Suzie's hand. She tried to pull herself up, but Lucy was too heavy hanging from her feet and the elevator abruptly tipped. I had a sudden, vertigo-inducing view straight down into the dark void of the spite's mouth as Suzie slipped out of my sweaty palm.

Their screams lasted only a brief moment before they were swallowed whole by the spite. The elevator tipped the other way, slamming me into the wall where I clung to the railing, eyes clenched tight again. I was alone. And terrified. My family and friends were gone. Eaten. I braced myself for the end as the spite's piercing screeches echoed in my ears. It shook the elevator and pressed its face to the door opening. I could feel its breath and smell its desperation. But it must not have seen me clinging to the corner because the next thing I knew, I was tumbling through the air.

The elevator crashed to the ground and rolled to a stop in the clearing.

I opened my eyes. Everything hurt. And there was blood on my face. I was pretty sure I'd broken my nose. I crawled out of the open door onto the dark, cool grass, disorientated and dizzy. I tried to stand up, but fell over and vomited instead. My chest was tight and my heart was racing; my eyes were watering and my mind was spinning. My whole body was trembling. I tried to move, but my stomach heaved again and again, though nothing else came up. I was having a full-blown panic attack. I started to crawl, desperate to find someplace safe, someplace where I could think, where I could breathe. I found a tree snapped in half by the spite and pulled myself against it. I turned round to face the clearing. The spite was still rampaging through the remains of the Lab 257 building, looking for other people to eat.

The elevator was about fifty feet away. It was crumpled like used tinfoil. I couldn't believe I survived. I couldn't believe I was the only one left. My therapist once warned me not to let my anxieties and emotions consume me, but everyone I loved was gone, consumed by the thing our collective anger and irritation had created. No matter what genetically modified amoebas it had originated from, the spite was ours. It was all of us.

The spite was me.

And once again, I found myself alone with my issues.

Just me and my monster.

I was frozen in fear, staring at the creature as it rose up on its hind legs to its full, towering height. I could just barely make out the dark shapes of all the people it had consumed and I knew I'd be joining them soon. I wanted to cry. My instinct was to fall apart, to run away. My body was prepping to self-destruct.

But then something clicked in my thought spiral. I remembered the smug look on Pauline Salt's face inside the spite. She didn't look dead; she just looked stuck. A thought broke through my panic: *My family is in there. My friends are in there. Innocent people are in there. And they might still be alive.* And then I saw it. Lying on the ground in the clearing between the spite and me.

The dart gun.

My blood started pumping hard; my breath was heavy. There was adrenaline coursing through my body; a surge of panic the likes of which I had never felt before. My anxiety disorder always made my fight-or-flight reactions kick in unnecessarily. But that wasn't the case this time. THIS was a necessary reaction. And that's when I realised it wasn't panic at all. It was *purpose*. I didn't feel overwhelmed; I felt like I was going to kill a spite.

What I needed was that dart gun. All that mattered was that dart gun. The only thing in the world besides me was that dart gun. I had to get it. I had to move. Survival mode. My body took over. My brain got overruled for once. Tunnel vision kicked in.

I stumbled forward, breaking into a shaky sprint as I entered the centre of the clearing. The spite turned just as I reached the elevator and scrambled round behind it. I peeked over the elevator and saw the spite looking away again.

I ran, as fast as I could, towards the spite and the dart gun. I tripped, fell and righted myself in one comically balletic move. "Get your poop together!" I shouted at myself – but most definitely did not say "poop". Given the situation, it felt only right to swear.

The spite heard me cursing and spun in my direction. It dropped onto all of its legs, shaking the ground, and was instantly on the move in my direction. I focused on the dart gun. It was close. Ten strides.

Five strides. And then I dived and rolled just as the spite swooped down with its gaping mouth. It missed me, but barely. Its face smushed into the spot where I had just been. I tumbled between its hundreds of legs as it passed over me.

I scrambled back to my feet at the edge of the clearing, where I spun to face the spite. The end of its body had compressed towards the front from the force of impact and its butt suddenly rebounded like an accordion in my direction. I backed away, frantic. Where was the dart gun? I couldn't see it anywhere. The spite must have crushed it. *You're a failure. This is all your fault,* I thought . . . until I looked down and saw the dart gun firmly gripped in my hand. How? Didn't matter. I had actually done it! My thought spiral could officially suck it.

The spite turned with a vicious, eardrum-exploding *SCREECH.* It could easily destroy me. I felt the panic rising again. My throat tightened. My heart felt like it was trying to break out of my chest. My hands shook; I could feel myself about to hyperventilate. But mini-victories are still victories: I had the dart gun. I could do this. I raised the weapon and cocked it loudly, just the way I had seen Dr Zanker do it in the elevator.

I felt scared.

And I felt brave.

It's possible to be both at once.

The spite narrowed its eyes. It screeched. I screamed. It ran at me. I aimed the dart gun, but held my fire. I waited for it to get closer.

Closer.

Closer.

Its mouth opened wide. Spite saliva slipped out. It was ready to swallow me down when I pulled the trigger and – *CLICK. CLICK. CLICK. CLICK.*

Nothing.

I pulled it again.

CLICK. CLICK. CLICK.

Something was missing: the fail-safe dart.

The spite lunged at me. I dived out of the way, but the spite anticipated that and it whipped its rear end out, sending me tumbling back into the clearing once more.

I realised what the ball in Wallyball felt like. Then I realised that I did not have the time to be thinking about that at all. I was really hurt, but I spat out the dirt and grass and blood and I pushed myself to my knees. It was still so dark. But I saw the slightest glimmer up ahead. A reflection of moonlight. The fail-safe dart was pressed into a patch of dirt beyond the grass, just a few feet away, where the gun had been earlier.

But my hands were empty again. *The gun! Where was the gun?* I thought. I must have lost my grip on it when the spite practically knocked me senseless. And I couldn't see it anywhere along the trail of torn-up grass I had just tumbled through. *How could it just disappear?!* I wondered. Then, as if on cue, the spite spat it out of its mouth from the edge of the clearing. It landed at my side, mangled and covered in slime and completely useless. It was like the spite was mocking me. But I wasn't done yet.

I'll stab it, was the only thought spinning through my mind.

I struggled to my feet. I fell. I was disorientated. Dizzy again. I may have had a concussion. So I crawled through the grass towards the dart. The spite moved slowly, like it knew it had me and was enjoying the hunt. It doubled back on itself, encircling me before closing in.

I got to the dart and dug it out of the ground, but as I picked it up, I realised the dart part was gone. It was just a glass vial. Without the dart or the gun, there was no way to inject it. The spite circled, closer and closer. The ground shook like the whole world was shivering. I crab-crawled backwards, but there was nowhere to go. The spite was everywhere. It was over: I was going to be spite food.

My life flashed before my eyes. Glimpses of my family, of Suzie, our house, my schools, all the doctors I'd seen and all the pills I'd taken. "You've taken so many pills, it's no wonder you've become one yourself," I remembered Lucy telling me the other day. I laughed. I was about to die and I laughed at the memory of this. She was right: I was a bit of a pill. And that's when it hit me. And I don't mean the spite.

"I *am* a pill," I blurted out loud.

The spite rose up, ready to pounce. But I wasn't looking at the spite; I was looking at the noxious vial of fail-safe in my hand. There was a hairline crack in the lip of it. I grabbed a rock and quickly cracked it open the rest of the way. The spite *SCREECHED*, its gaping, gooey mouth ready to feed. And just as it dived down for me, I doused myself in fail-safe.

And I let myself get eaten alive.

CHAPTER 19

THE RECOVERY

What happened next was incredibly unpleasant. I remember a sticky coldness inside the spite's mouth. I remember moving uncomfortably down into its gelatinous goo of a body like I was on the worst waterslide ever. My body became paralysed. My mind started to fade. It felt like falling asleep. And then I died.

At least that's what I thought happened. My mind went black. I had no thoughts. No feelings. Nothing.

I just wasn't there any more.

Until . . .

Something started shaking me like when Mom tries to wake me for school after I break my alarm and go back to bed. I realised, little by little, that I was going to have to open my eyes, but I really didn't want to. Then I heard a horrible *SCREECH*. I felt it rumble through me like a train on old tracks. It annoyed me. I was angry that I was being disturbed from my sleep. My eyes opened, reluctantly, finally, and I was confused at what I saw. It looked like the extreme close-ups of those amoebas we found in the lab. Like cells were dividing and pulling apart all around me. But then the goo really did start to pull apart. As I blinked my eyes clear, I saw the horrible face of a bugbear staring right at me. It *ROARED*. I screamed. And with a gooey, gross, gloppy sound, we both fell.

I landed hard on a sandy beach. Above me, as the sun was rising, the spite was being torn apart from the inside out. Its gooey particles breaking down into the hundreds of bugbears that had come together to form it in the first place.

It was actually pretty disgusting, which made sense because that was exactly how I felt. I was covered in sticky, smelly awfulness and sand. The spite must have wandered to the shore of the island while I was unconscious inside it. But then I heard an unexpected sound. "Slim?" It was Lucy. She was next to me in a pool of her own slime.

"Lucy!" I yelled, scrambling past the twitching, dying bugbears to hug her. "You're alive!" I said as she hugged me back.

"What happened?" she asked, suddenly aware that there were bugbears everywhere. They were dazed and trembling. They wandered aimlessly, trying to recombine back into the spite, but were unable to stick to each other.

"Slim? Lucy?" Mom and Dad shouted. They scooped us up before we'd even seen them. "You're okay. We're okay!" said Mom, hugging us so tightly I could barely breathe.

"How is this possible?" asked Dad. "It ate us! We were . . . gone."

I pulled away from the hug long enough to breathe and speak. "Lucy was right," I said, surprising them all. "I've taken so many pills that I became one myself."

"Clever boy," came the voice of Dr Zanker, examining the sticky goo that glazed his lab coat and the remnants of the broken vial of fail-safe. "You covered yourself in the fail-safe? Not the safest way to administer the dosage, but clearly effective."

Mom and Dad grabbed me by the shoulders as if they were about to punish me. "You *let* the spite eat you?" they shouted.

"It was the only way to stop it," I said. "It was the only way to get you back."

"You were the cure," came another voice I was relieved to hear. I turned to see Suzie with her dads. They were holding her close. I smiled, too delirious from all the action to be nervous around Suzie any more.

"And I'm all natural too," I added.

Suzie smiled and said, "I really like all-natural products." I almost passed out. Suzie Minkle just said she liked me. Sort of. Right? That's what she meant. But did that mean she like-liked me too?

There was an audible gasp and we turned to see Pauline Salt next to General Esposito and the rest of the soldiers. She coughed into her fist and spat out spite goo and then stumbled to her feet, straightening her slime-covered power suit. "What happened?" she asked, just before spotting the bugbears down by the waves. "Bugbears!" she screamed, slipping in the slime as she tried to scramble away and face-planting in the sand.

"They aren't aggressive at the moment," said Dr Zanker as he walked over to examine one, right past Ms Salt as she was standing up unsteadily. "The fail-safe is a sort of reverse-PVZ. It was designed to undo the effects, so I imagine it's breaking down their cellular make-up as we speak." He poked a bugbear, getting his finger stuck in it to emphasise his point. The bugbear just sort of looked over at Dr Zanker before shoving him away with one of its legs, knocking him into Pauline Salt, who fell again and got her second faceful of sand.

"What are you all talking about?" came the authoritative and totally frustrated voice of General Esposito. "What bugbears? There's nothing here," he said, looking all around us at his troops and then down at the slime he was covered in, asking, "And what the hell is all over us?" I guess even being stuck inside the spite didn't mean he could actually see any of the PVZ-spawned creatures. He was still never exposed to the original airborne PVZ. But as he leaned into his shoulder radio, requesting backup, I realised he was accidentally right about one thing. The bugbears weren't technically there any more. They were dissolving right before our eyes, just like the spite had.

The bugbears practically melted to the ground, reduced to slime, releasing all the peeves and people they'd consumed. That's when I heard a familiar sniffle. But it wasn't Sniffle Peeve. It was Otis Miller. He got up, confused and sniffling like he always did. He wiped the slime out of his eyes and looked at me and then at the slime he was covered in and then back at me. And all he could say was, "Do you have a tissue?"

Then came the peeves. Like an unruly wave. And I laughed, surprised at how excited I was to see them. There were thousands of them. And they instantly started doing whatever they were born to do. It was total mayhem. I couldn't help but laugh. My family and the Minkles did too. I could only imagine what General Esposito and his recovering soldiers must have thought, watching us.

"After everything we've been through, to think it was just these little guys that started it all," said Mom.

"Yeah, they really don't seem that bad right now, do they?" agreed Dad. It was nice to see them not making a big deal out of little things any more.

"Does anyone see Asking Peeve?" I asked, trying to spot the curious little fur ball amid the chaos.

Dr Zanker walked through the peeves, examining them one at a time. "The cellular make-up of the spite must have kept us in some form of frozen animation. Perhaps it was using us to fuel its energy supply, in much the same way these peeves seem to thrive off the annoyance they cause us," he said, utterly fascinated. "It will require further study, of course." Which was met with disdainful looks from the rest of us.

"That will depend on how well I can spin this for the board members," said Pauline Salt as she kicked peeves away from her. "I'm no longer convinced that being liability-free is a reasonable goal."

I thought I saw Asking Peeve, but it was just another furry blue peeve that turned round and burped really loudly. Dr Zanker picked it up to examine it, but as he did, the peeve disintegrated before our eyes. "Ah, yes. The fail-safe is reversing the PVZ right down to its origins," observed Dr Zanker. And he was right. I looked around and saw the horde of peeves dissolving down into what must have been the original PVZ amoebas. And I have to admit, it broke my heart a little bit. I'd never get to thank Asking Peeve for saving our lives.

"I actually feel bad for the peeves," I said. "It wasn't their fault they evolved into a spite. They didn't ask for this."

Lucy looked over at me. "Sounds familiar," she said with a sympathetic nudge. I wasn't used to anyone else understanding what I go through. But I have to say it felt pretty good.

I took a deep breath, inhaling the saltwater air, and I closed my eyes, listening to the calming sound of the ocean waves hitting the shore. The tide rushed up around my ankles, cleaning the sticky remnants of PVZ off my feet, and off the rest of the beach, washing it away for ever.

"Well, that solves a lot of my problems," said Pauline Salt, finally regaining some semblance of composure.

"Yes," added Dr Zanker, far less enthused about the

peeves' demise. "I suppose this particular experiment has officially ended," he said, fumbling in his lab coat pockets. And I swear I caught a glimpse of him palming the spray bottle of PVZ from Lab 257 as he hurried off into the crowd of confused people who'd just woken up, slime-covered, on a beach they definitely wouldn't remember coming to.

"Can we go home now?" asked Lucy.

"Yes," said Mom and Dad at the same time before looking over at each other, unsure which home they were talking about. The Minkles were splashing in the surf, enjoying the moment, happy to be alive, and rather than argue about whose turn it was or which home we'd go to, we looked at each other, shrugged, and joined them – Mom, Dad, Lucy and me. Splashing in the water and jumping the waves. It was like my "medication vacation" had transformed into an actual one. It might have been the best family vacation we ever had.

I slipped in the surf and Suzie reached out to help me up. But she didn't let go when I was back on my feet. And this wasn't just a reflex in the moment. She wasn't afraid for me. How do I know? Because this time she leaned in and kissed my cheek. Yep, she like-liked me. My heart started to race and my face flushed. But this wasn't a panic attack. This was a totally normal reaction to a new and unexpected stimulus. I smiled and she smiled back. And then I really surprised myself. I took a deep breath and leaned in to give her a real kiss, which would have made for a picture-perfect ending.

If not for the Black Hawk helicopters filled with armed Homeland Security forces descending upon us instead.

CHAPTER 20

THE RESULTS MAY VARY

BEEP. BEEP. BEEP. BEEP.

The sound was still the worst. My alarm clock ripped me awake. I stared at it for a beat, allowing the sound to exist without letting it get the best of me. I reached out and turned it off as if this were just another normal day. For a moment, I wondered if it was all just a crazy dream.

"Slim! Get up and get ready!" called Mom from downstairs just as Lucy walked into my room without knocking. I sat up and rubbed the sleep out of my eyes, stretching my sore body.

"Here's your iPad," said Lucy, holding the tablet she swore she hadn't "borrowed" last week. "Sorry I took it without asking," she continued. I blinked at her in confusion as she sat on the edge of my bed, tapping at the screen. "But check it out," she said. "Our town is famous!"

She pulled up a streaming news site. A reporter

stood in front of the rubble of Old Wayford Town Hall. "The CDC still has no answers for the inexplicable outbreak of mass hysteria in Old Wayford, which seems to have ended just as quickly as it began," said the reporter, confirming, if I ever really doubted it, that I did not dream any of it.

The video showed handheld clips of the peeves and bugbears rampaging through town, and even the spite forming in the distance by Clarity Labs, but the reporter still concluded, "Though residents tell us that 'monsters' attacked Old Wayford, there remains no visual evidence to corroborate the claims. The seemingly inexplicable destruction on view is being blamed on unusual wind activity, though no hurricane or tornado was officially reported. A CDC spokesperson suggests that local water supplies may have been tainted by an accident at Clarity Labs, causing a mass delusion that led to mass hysteria. A fire subsequently destroyed Clarity Labs, along with any real proof of what may have caused it. Clarity Labs CEO Pauline Salt has issued a statement saying the pharmaceutical giant will take full responsibility for any damages that may have been caused by this unfortunate incident, if liability can be proven."

The screen lit up with a text from Suzie. It read,

"That was a really weird first date, huh?" And it was followed by a winking-face emoji.

I smiled like a goof and Lucy rolled her eyes. "You can talk to your girlfriend later," she said as she turned the iPad off. "All these, like, official officials have actually been questioning people in town to find out if we're still 'seeing' monsters — like we were all hallucinating and caused the damage ourselves," she said in disbelief.

"Sometimes it's easier to pretend you're okay when you really aren't," I told her. "But we know better, right?" I said as I gave her a playful shove.

"Right," she said, shoving me back.

"Ow! Don't. Everything hurts," I moaned as I rubbed the bruise she accidentally hit.

"Mom wants us downstairs," Lucy said. "We're going to meet up with Dad and figure out what to do with the old house. Or what's left of it," she added as she carefully made her way out of my messy room.

My Spider-Man poster had fallen off the wall again, just like it did after I kicked Telling Peeve into it. I pinned it back where it belonged before stumbling over yesterday's dirty clothes. But instead of just leaving them there, I stopped and picked them up and tossed them in the laundry basket. It was a simple thing to do, but I knew it would keep Mom from getting upset, which would prevent her from bugging me about it, which would prevent Lucy from having something to tell on me for, which would prevent Dad from being blamed for it after the fact.

As I tried to tidy up the rest of my room, I caught a glimpse of myself in my mirror. If I needed any further proof that it all really happened, my bruised and bandaged head would suffice. I was poking at my broken nose, wondering how long it would take to heal when I heard a crumpling sound behind me and saw the Spider-Man poster had fallen again. I picked it up and tried to pin it back where it belonged, but then I noticed that my cubby door was open a crack. For a moment, I imagined I'd find it filled with peeves and almost got excited about it. But when I pulled it open, it was just the same old safe space from before – pillows and blankets, an almost-empty container of Twizzlers, and my comics. After everything I went through yesterday, I wondered if I'd ever feel the need to sit in there again. I shook my head and told myself, "Just keep your poop together, Slim."

"Who are you talking to?" came a familiar voice behind me.

"Just talking to myself, Lu . . ." but I trailed off

because Lucy wasn't in my room. In fact, there was no one there at all. Then I felt a tapping on my foot and looked down to see Asking Peeve. It was looking up at me with those totally innocent, totally curious eyes. I couldn't believe it.

I scooped it up and gave it the biggest hug. "Where did you come from? How did you get here? Didn't you get eaten?" I asked, rapid-fire. I put Asking Peeve on my bed. It appeared to be confused. "Aren't I supposed to be asking the questions?" it asked. I had to laugh. I couldn't believe it was alive – and I couldn't believe I was so happy about that.

"Am I still bad?" it asked in the tiniest little voice. And that's when I realised exactly why I was so happy. Asking Peeve is just a little, furry, living version of my ability to question myself and the world around me. It's not a bad thing – in fact it may be the only way to ever really learn anything at all. But still, I understood that feeling of being bad just because I was being me all too well. So I looked it right in the eyes and said in the most reassuring tone I could muster, "You risked your own life to save ours. You were never bad. You were just . . . you. Like me."

Asking Peeve smiled, really happy to hear that. "What about the others?" it asked.

I furrowed my brow. "What others?"

And that's when I heard a telltale sniffle and saw Sniffle Peeve crawl out from under the bed, wiping its nose on one of my socks. Then Crazy Peeve sprang out of the laundry basket where I had just thrown my dirty clothes, shouting, "Grun grun doobie blah!"

I was so confused. "But how did you survive? I thought the bugbear got you."

"The safe space," came another familiar voice. It was Telling Peeve, crawling out from under a pillow in the cubby. "You didn't see us escape and run all the way here to be safe," it explained. Which was true, now that I thought about it. We had barricaded ourselves inside the old house while these guys were chased down by bugbears outside. I just assumed they were gone. And I never actually saw the bugbear grab Asking Peeve either − they were both enveloped in rubble dust and only the bugbear emerged as we drove away.

"You were never exposed to the fail-safe liquid, so you didn't dissolve like the others," I realised. "You're the only peeves left!"

"Slim! Hurry! Your father is waiting," came the call from Mom downstairs.

"Where are you going?" asked Asking Peeve.

"To clean up the mess at our old home, I guess," I replied.

Asking Peeve thought for a moment, and then wanted to know, "Is this your home now?"

I sort of shrugged. "One of them," was the best I could offer. Asking Peeve nodded, as if it understood. Then it looked troubled and asked, "Is this OUR home now?"

I was so surprised to see them again that it hadn't even dawned on me. What was I going to do with four little peeves? They were lost and alone in a world that doesn't understand them. I really did relate. And even though Sniffle Peeve would probably never get rid of that runny nose and Crazy Peeve would probably never do or say anything that made sense, it wasn't their fault. It was just who they are.

I could hear Mom coming up the stairs, and I wasn't sure yet if she should know about them. "That's your home," I said, pointing to the safe space. The peeves got super excited and ran into the cubby. I closed it just as Mom walked in. She looked at my floor, happily surprised to see it wasn't covered in clothes.

"Come on, sweetie. We have a lot to do today," she said before hesitating. "Are you okay? I mean, minus the injuries. You look a little—"

But I cut her off before she could finish her thought. "I'm never really totally okay, Mom, but I'm better today than I was yesterday." Which was true. Maybe for the first time ever.

She walked over and gave me a kiss on the head, which I naturally grimaced at and shrank away from. "All right, all right," she said. "Just hurry up. Dad's already at the house with the crew. And don't think I've forgotten about your candy stash. I still don't think you should be eating so much sugar. And leaving food in here will totally attract pests. Which reminds me . . ." she said as she walked through the door calling out, "Lucy, about that little 'borrowing' habit of yours . . ."

Despite being busted, it was kind of nice to know that things were going back to normal. I opened the cubby, finding the peeves happily making themselves at home.

"You're in *our* home," said Telling Peeve, pointing a half-eaten Twizzler at me.

"I guess I am," I said, happy to see it finding another use. "This is *your* safe space now."

I felt a tug at my sleeve and Asking Peeve wondered, "What happens next?"

I really didn't have a good answer for that. I ruffled

its furry little head, but all I could offer was, "We'll just have to wait and see." And that's when Crazy Peeve tore a pillow apart in its excitement, sending feathers everywhere. Sniffle Peeve sneezed and reached for my sleeve to wipe its nose, but then seemed to think twice and wiped it on a blanket instead. It was a start.

When my therapist suggested that Mom and Dad get me an emotional support animal, I'm pretty sure this wasn't what she had in mind. But life is weird and unpredictable and now I have several of these . . . pets.

"Pet peeves," I said, realising that this was what they had just become.

"What's a *pet* peeve?" asked Asking Peeve.

"We are," answered Telling Peeve. "And that means he has to take care of us!" it declared, pointing at me as the other peeves settled into their new home, embracing their newfound identities.

"I have actual pet peeves," I said again.

And I know I'm not the only one. You probably have your own pet peeves in some form or another. Mine just happen to be very, very real. And they may never totally go away, but I guess that's true for everyone, in a sense. There will always be annoying things in the world. That won't ever change. So it's up to me to find better ways of dealing with them. And to maybe also try harder to understand that other people are dealing with peeves of their own.

But here's the thing I've learned about other people's peeves: you can't ever actually see them. You can only see their reaction to them. I'm going to do my best to keep mine in check. I'm going to try not to overreact to them any more. In fact, I'm just going to have to figure out how to live with them.

Literally.

I'm not sure if any of this made sense to you, but that's not really the point. The point is that it makes sense to me. And sometimes we need to let other people know what we see and think and feel, whether they see or think or feel those same things or not. Before all of this happened, I definitely wasn't doing much to help myself. But I've actually been giving my therapist a real shot lately. I don't know if she really believes me about any of this, but she listens. And even if she doesn't believe me, at least I know I have a family and friends who understand. Because they've been through it too.

That's why I'm sharing my story. It's not easy to do. But I learned the hard way that if you let your peeves loose, they could evolve into bigger, badder monsters that will literally eat you alive . . . or maybe just figuratively, if you've never been exposed to PVZ. But either way, if you're dealing with peeves or anxieties or fears or any overwhelming feelings of your own, I want you to know that you're not alone. Even if you feel like you are. I'm right there with you, going through all the weird stuff and feeling all the weird things and sometimes feeling really alone even when there are people around too. It's all pretty confusing, but the cool thing is that everyone else is pretty confused too.

When you really think about it, I guess we're all just lab rats in the science experiment of life. But we can do something that actual lab rats can't do: we can talk. And we can write. And we can draw and sing and even make videos that help us find people who think and feel the same way we do. We can connect with each other.

So the next time something is really bothering you, and you don't know how to handle it, or feel totally alone with it, don't be afraid to share your feelings.

It's a whole lot better than being eaten by them.

Trust me.

EPILOGUE:

THE VIRAL FACTOR

"So the next time something is really bothering you, and you don't know how to handle it, or feel totally alone with it, don't be afraid to share your feelings. It's a whole lot better than being eaten by them. Trust me," concluded the weird kid on one of those viral videos that had been going around since the "incident" in Old Wayford.

"Talia, you *have* to watch this. It happened last autumn, just a couple of towns over!" said my cousin Denny, who fell down a monster-hunting YouTube hole at the beginning of the week.

Spring break was finally coming to a merciful end. My family calls it camping, but it felt like we'd been marooned at this state park for ages. I guess it's nice to dip my toes in the ocean, but I'm always freaked out that some crab is gonna pinch me and, honestly, I can't sleep with all this quiet.

At least Denny's Wi-Fi hot spot worked and we

could get online out here. "Do you think they really saw invisible monsters?" asked Denny, a little too eagerly. I mean, this made for entertaining YouTube-ing, but come on.

"It's just a hoax," I told him. "The whole town probably got together to plan this flash-mob version of a monster attack just to go viral and boost tourism."

Denny shrugged and poked at a tiny jellyfish thing with a stick. We'd seen a bunch of them washing up this morning, which was yet another reason I was excited to head home today. "He just turned his *Dear Evan Hansen* issues into a monster mash. And what kind of a name is Slim Pickings anyway? Totally made up," I concluded.

"Yeah, you're probably right." Denny sighed. "Maybe we should make our own viral video!" he added, flinging those jellyfish things at me and laughing from behind his camera phone as I squealed and squirmed on screen, using my backpack as a shield.

"Ugh. You are SO ANNOYING!" I shouted and stormed off the beach.

Denny made a GIF out of that clip and sent it to me later, when I was safely back in our apartment in the city. I'd definitely had enough nature for the year.

But the text he sent with the GIF read, "IT MOVED!"

At first I didn't know what he was talking about because it's a video and of course it moved. But then I looked closer at the clip. One of the tiny jellyfish things was darker. Almost black. More like a goo. And as soon as I told Denny how annoying he is, I swear . . . that black goo moved.

Right into the backpack now sitting at the foot of my bed.

ACKNOWLEDGEMENTS

First and foremost, I'd like to thank everyone who has ever annoyed me, without whom, none of this would have been possible. But feel free to stop now.

This idea started as a doodle almost a decade ago, and I never really expected it to become anything more than that. And it may have never evolved this way without the encouragement of my manager Zac Frognowski, who supports all of my weird ideas. I'm also lucky to have a great team of agents in Joe Mann, Trevor Astbury, Cait Hoyt and Michelle Weiner, whose hard work made this project a reality.

But this is a book, and up until now I've only written screenplays. So I'm incredibly grateful to my editor David Linker for seeing the potential in an unformed concept from a guy who had never written a book before and for having the patience and energy to shepherd it along. And another big thank you goes to the entire HarperCollins team for helping to shape this book into something I can be proud to see on bookshelves and beyond. I literally could not have done it without you.

Peeves is a story about overwhelming thoughts and feelings, the importance of mental health, and the struggle to connect with those who are different from you. As someone who lives with anxiety, depression and has faced chronic health issues, I know the value and challenge of advocating for one's own wellbeing. To that end, I need to acknowledge every doctor, therapist and wellness practitioner from Eastern to Western approaches who has played or continues to play a part in keeping my mind and body as sound as possible. It's a tricky endeavor, but I appreciate all of your efforts in helping to keep my "poop" together.

It's also important to recognise my emotional support system for sticking with me through it all. Mom, Dad, Jeff, Mark, Gigi and Kate – you've always done your best to help, comfort and encourage me even when you don't understand whatever it is I'm going through or working on now, and I love you for it. The same goes for my found family, Erin Rodman, Ross Maxwell, Steve Yockey, Ben Roy, Kacie Kane, Betsy Megel and Camille Chen, who have all played pivotal parts in my growth as a writer and a person.

And, finally, I want to thank Aaron Hartzler for the writers' retreat where I finished the first draft of this book, Christian Anderson for building me the Asking Peeve puppet I never had to use during the movie pitch I never had to give, Andrea McCall for my first job in creative development, Cindy Levinson for those early days as a writer, Alison Small for believing in my work, Jeff Blitz for the script notes and validation along the way, and Allen Clary for passing my scripts to his agents, which started a domino effect of unpredictable events that ultimately landed me here.

It's been an exciting and rewarding experience bringing this book to life and I feel very lucky to have the opportunity to share a little piece of my personal weirdness with any reader who picks it up. If you happen to be one of those readers, and you've made it all the way to the end of these acknowledgements after reading this whole silly story, then thank you for your support as well. I really hope you enjoyed it! (But if you didn't, please feel free to file your complaints with Snarky Peeve. I'm sure it will have a very fair and balanced response for you.)